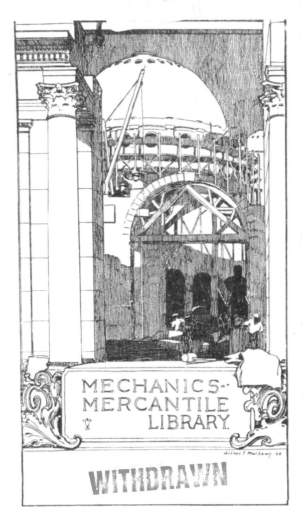

MECHANICS··
MERCANTILE
LIBRARY.

MIDNIGHT GUARDIANS

Previous Titles in the Max Freeman series by Jonathon King

THE BLUE EDGE OF MIDNIGHT
A VISIBLE DARKNESS
SHADOW MEN
A KILLING NIGHT
ACTS OF NATURE

MIDNIGHT GUARDIANS

A Max Freeman Thriller

Jonathon King

severn
House

This first world hardcover edition published 2011
in Great Britain and in the USA by
SEVERN HOUSE PUBLISHERS LTD of
9–15 High Street, Sutton, Surrey, England, SM1 1DF.
eBook edition first published in the USA 2010 by
Open Road Integrated Media.

British Library Cataloguing in Publication Data

King, Jonathon.
  Midnight guardians.
  1. Freeman, Max (Fictitious character)--Fiction.
  2. Ex-police officers--Florida--Fiction. 3. Medicare
  fraud--Florida--Fiction. 4. Suspense fiction.
  I. Title
  813.6-dc22

ISBN-13: 978-0-7278-8105-2 (cased)

All Severn House titles are printed on acid-free paper.

Severn House Publishers support The Forest Stewardship Council [FSC],
the leading international forest certification organisation. All our titles that
are printed on Greenpeace-approved FSC-certified paper carry the FSC logo.

Printed and bound in Great Britain by
MPG Books Ltd., Bodmin, Cornwall.

For Kath and a new beginning

Acknowledgments

I wish to thank my agent, Philip Spitzer, who got me this gig; all the people at Open Road Media bravely jumping into this new era of publishing; and the truly dedicated prosecutors and members of law enforcement working to end rampant fraud and close the pill mills in my beloved state of Florida.

1

YOU SHOULD HAVE seen it coming—been smarter. Been quicker. Been wiser.

But it always works like that, doesn't it? It's only after the fact that you start looking at it from that useless "what if" viewpoint. *What if* you'd seen the signs? *What if* you'd done things differently? *What if* you'd seen it coming and avoided having your legs sheared off by five thousand pounds of speeding metal?

Why couldn't you see it was all working backward that night? You always liked the night shift, the change in people, the way they walked different, talked different, and looked different: the way they eased up from their daytime drudgery and let loose a little bit. It was at night that people dropped the layer of inhibition that made them a bunch of boring civilians. Working the night shift was always better than punching the clock in the daytime world, with all its mind-numbing rules and procedures.

The other upside is that nighttime is also when the street criminals come out. The same darkness and shadows that make regular folks feel a little more obscure also spike up the chance of shit hitting the fan. As a cop, you can have a little fun busting some asshole for breaking and entering, or holding up a Stop and Rob, or actually attempting a real rape down on the beachfront. But any patrol cop will also tell you that despite the so-called crime rate, real shit doesn't happen nearly enough in one guy's sector to keep the boredom from creeping up your spine and making you wiggle your ass in the seat of the car, or making you wanna just get out and run a few laps on the empty high school track under the security lights, or prop your toes up on the front bumper of the patrol car and do a hundred push-ups on the parking lot in front of Fire Engine Company No. 5. You know those pussies are inside watching you from their cushy break room, and that there's no way they're gonna come outside and get challenged on how many reps they can do.

So you're cool with the night shift. But that night, it was all god-damned backward. And you didn't see it coming.

Instead of covering your usual sector, you were gonna have to shift gears, because the local highway patrol division was short three troopers. The sergeant told you that you had to drive out of the neighborhoods and do a few runs down I-595, 'cause there'd been some bullshit reporting of speed gunners doing hundred-mile-an-hour blow-downs from the tollbooth at the entrance of Alligator Alley; some poor civilian might freak out and get whammed in the contest. Yeah, whatever.

Now instead of creeping the streets, you were doing the opposite, laying a speed trap on the interstate, cruising the inside lane at fifty-five m.p.h., and occasionally pulling off onto the shoulder with the lights off, waiting—being bored out of your fucking mind. No speeders. No high-speed chase—just the opposite. Nobody's shooting more than five or ten m.p.h. over the posted limit, and what the hell, you ain't wasting your time running *them* down. So you pop some super protein tabs and crank up the iPod, which is completely against the rules, and you're listening to some good old classic AC/DC when there in the rearview is some driver whose got to be doing thirty-five m.p.h. in the middle lane, screwing everybody up.

You're watching, and it makes you cringe just to see how slow this idiot's going. Then just as the car passes, you see the driver's profile: one of those old white-hairs leaning toward the windshield, eyes squinting and nose nearly touching the steering wheel as though that extra six inches is going to allow her to see a hundred feet further down the road. And then you hear the horn of the guy coming up behind her, who has been fooled by the taillights of her old Lincoln Town Car. Unexpectedly, those lights come racing up into his face, he hits the horn as he swerves past the old lady, and there goes that *yeeeeeowwww* of sound that gets bent by the Doppler effect.

Shit! Now you've got to do something, right? You are out here with the fucking mandate to stop accidents from happening, right?

So you pull the iPod buds out of your ears, and on go your headlights. On go the spinning blues on the light bar, and out you pull onto the interstate to catch up to Miss Marple. Everything is backward. You're not chasing some hopped-up nineteen-year-old flier; you're stopping your grandmother for going too slow.

Cussing, you push the patrol car to fifty m.p.h. to catch up. For now, you stay off the siren, not wanting to scare the shit out of the old lady. You slow up just behind her and slide just to her outside mirror so she can't miss the spinning lights now flashing into her car's interior and making everything pulsate in blue, even her white hair. Sure enough, she doesn't slow down a bit. Other cars around and behind you are slowing because they can see the damn lights. And like most drivers in the world, their natural tendency is to slow down when they see a cop, because God forbid they did something wrong, or were running ten miles over the limit themselves. So they all slow down for thirty seconds. But once they see it's somebody else getting yanked, they all jack it back up to seventy.

You know this is true because you're a cop and you know the paranoia you invoke. And you're kind of proud of it. But what the hell is wrong with this old biddy, who's not stopping or even slowing down but instead sticking to thirty-five m.p.h. like her life depended on it.

Then you think: God, I hope this isn't one of those Chicken Little, the sky is falling, dipshits who's heard the story of the fake officer who pulls people over with a red light on their dash, and then rapes and robs them. OK, you've heard it, too, but never with any detail as to what jurisdiction and exactly what was threatened, or specifically what was stolen. You're not sure it isn't just one of those urban legends, like the alligators in the sewer and the boa constrictor in the toilet plumbing. But shit, this broad ain't reacting at all.

So against all rules of procedure, you finally get frustrated, flick on the siren, and pull around in front of the Town Car and slow down yourself, using this maneuver to make her stop behind you. See what I mean? Backward—just fucking backward.

Now you get out. And against the shine of her headlights, you shade your eyes and walk back to her vehicle. You're absolutely second-guessing why the hell you even decided to do this, thinking you should have just let her get rear-ended and not wasted your time. But you do, without malice or forethought, just by habit, have your right hand resting on the butt of your 9 mm. Maybe that's why the old girl is already crying, with her hands raised up into the fabric ceiling of the Town Car, pleading in a high hysterical voice, "Please, Officer, please don't shoot me. I'm sorry. I'm sorry. I was just trying to get to the airport to pick up my daughter. I didn't mean to be unlawful. I'm sorry! Please don't shoot me!"

"It's OK, ma'am. It's OK," you're saying, now showing her the palms of both of your hands and spreading your fingers and flapping them down with that international sign language to just calm the fuck down.

"Take it easy," you say. "I'm just trying to help you, ma'am. Please."

As you bend to show your face in her window, you see the watery blue eyes and the tension in the wrinkled forehead and the flaccid muscles of her arms shaking with the effort to keep her hands up.

"Please, ma'am. You can put your hands down, please. Just let me see your driver's license and registration, please," you say, now falling back into procedural mode and realizing that you haven't done due diligence by calling in the tag number before making the stop. Now you have to rectify your own miscue.

"I was only concerned, ma'am, that you might be having trouble negotiating the freeway. It is dark, ma'am, and traffic moves fairly briskly along this stretch of road. I was afraid you were traveling at a dangerously slow rate, uh, Mrs. Mitchell," you say, now looking at the license, which is a renewal she's probably received through the mail for the last forty years without having to take an eye or reflex test. Her date of birth, you can now see, is 1936.

So after telling her to please stay in the car, you walk around to the back of her vehicle. Backward, right? What the fuck were you thinking? No cop in his right mind makes a traffic stop with his lights spinning *in front* of the vehicle he's pulled over. But you stand there behind her Town Car, jotting down the license tag number, and then you hear something that registers ever so slightly in the synapses of your brain. The sound of upcoming traffic has changed. And the spray of light from the headlights behind you also changes. Suddenly, the ambient light has instantly decreased by one degree.

You hear the upcoming whine of engine before you see the car. Out of your peripheral vision, the front of an older model grill, the big chromed-up steel ones they used when cars were still solid and heavy, is rushing up in the pull-over lane. The car's headlights are off. You perceive only a winking reflection in the old grillwork, and you have just a millisecond to turn to face the onrushing steel. Since you're an excellent athlete, your instant reaction is to try and jump.

You do not hear the impact. Your brain shuts down—all black. All silent, an automatic response by the organism, they tell you later, a response to what your animal system tells you is instant death.

2

"JESUS," I SAID, and not in the cynical way I usually take the Lord's name in vain, but with a true amount of awe and sympathy. "He was pinned?"

"When the first highway patrol troopers got there, they could see him in their headlights," Sherry said. "His torso was still straight up, not slumped over the hood or anything. They said his head was back and his mouth wide open, like he was yelling to the sky. But he wasn't making a sound."

"Jesus," I said again, putting the image in my head, and then having a hard time shaking it out. Maybe Sherry could sense my discomfort, or maybe she just went back to concentrating on the macadam roadway, because she went silent for a while. She hadn't even gotten to the point of why she was telling me the tale.

All that came out of her now was that rhythmic breathing and the almost imperceptible grunt of effort each time she pushed the wheels of her wheelchair, spinning them forward, her wrists feathering up like a rower does when he's finishing a stroke in a skull. Her chair would glide for a second while she exhaled, re-cocking her arms and preparing to spin again.

I was riding next to her, peddling in a middle gear on a ten-speed touring bike. When we'd first started coming out here to Shark Valley in the southern Everglades, I actually jogged next to her while she rode the chair. She wouldn't let me push her—never had. Even the day she left the hospital, only a week after having her leg amputated, she refused to let anyone push her wheelchair.

Then after two days at home, she decided to take herself down the ramp I'd built off her back porch. She figured out a way to open the wooden gate herself, and was rolling down the street "to breathe some fresh air, for God's sake, Max," she'd snapped when I'd asked what the hell she thought she was doing. "That room, the house, the walls. It's like being in a freaking cell up at Raiford."

I'd started to say something about her not knowing what being in a Florida State Prison cell was truly like, even though she'd sent more than a few convicts up the line as a detective with the Broward Sheriff's Office. But I'd learned to keep my mouth shut at such times. Sherry had lost her leg during a camping trip I'd taken her on in the Glades. I'd been ignorant of a churning hurricane in the lower gulf. Then I'd soaked our only cell phone in a stupid move to dunk her playfully.

After her leg was shattered in the storm, I was the one who'd led us into a spider's nest of criminal assholes, putting both of us in jeopardy. The fishing shack we'd gone to wasn't what it appeared to be—not to us, or to the idiots who were looting camps after the storm. When armed muscle for the real owners showed up, we got caught in the crossfire. The result was the loss of Sherry's limb. I would never forgive myself.

So what Sherry Richards wanted to do these days, we did. If she wanted to get out of the house, I brought her here, a peaceful six-mile loop of macadam off the old Tamiami Trail on which folks could ride through a true Everglades meadow. To me, it was breathtaking: green-gold saw grass spread out to the horizon and lit by a rising sun in the morning, standing lakes of shallow water in the rainy season rippling in the wind and alive at times with hovering dragonflies and darters and the occasional bream that scooped up the insects from below. When I'd point out these marvels of nature to Sherry as we cruised along, I got mostly an uninterested nod. Such observances were not her idea of breathtaking anymore.

The first time we came out here, I'd walked alongside her, both of us breathing the humid, earth-cleaned air. I watched her carefully to make sure she didn't overheat in the South Florida sun. I carried lots of water and kept my cell phone in my pocket, ready at all times. I'd had to jog to keep up with her and drank most of the water myself. The next trip,

I ran the entire six-mile loop; she was waiting for me at the end. Finally, I rented a bike, and we'd been doing it that way ever since. Sherry was a triathlete before her amputation. Now she was a driven, disabled triathlete with a chip on her shoulder.

I'd told myself a thousand times in the last six months to let it go, let her work it out, let her master it; then she'll return to who she was. Neither one of us is going to be twenty-five again, but neither wanted to give up a workout, either. She'd made two concessions so far: She agreed to wear a big, floppy hat to shade her blonde head, and she took her trainer's advice not to push so hard that she couldn't carry on a conversation while wheeling.

She chose the Marty Booker story. Booker was a fellow sheriff's officer who'd lost both legs during a routine traffic stop on I-595. And why she was telling me the story? She'd been asked to meet with Booker, to talk with him, to counsel him. I was just happy not to have been the one giving her that assignment.

"The captain and one of the department psychs thought it would be a good idea. It's the old 'brothers-in-arms' drill: You've been through what he's going to have to go through. You'll have a reference point. Maybe you can help him," Sherry finally went on.

"I didn't see anybody helping you," I said, trying to be on her side, even though I knew the only reason she hadn't had a counselor or therapist or shrink to lean on when she was rehabbing, was that she was stubbornly adamant that she'd didn't need help.

"Yeah, well, they're saying he's having a hard time adjusting. Way too distracted and quiet and internal. He's not opening up at all, even to family. So they're thinking one crip cop to another, maybe we can connect."

"And you agreed," I said, maybe letting a tinge of surprise sneak into my voice: Sherry as therapist and a sounding board? Not her style.

"I heard stories about the guy before he got hit. He was too wild, too into himself, too much of that 'cop as soldier' stuff. Who needs that in their squad?" Sherry said. "But now, you know, he's a wheelie like me. I'm thinking maybe it's not a bad idea to talk to him."

That said, she exhaled and did the silent thing again. *Whoosh,* glide. *Whoosh,* glide. *Whoosh,* glide. Not a word. Over the last few months, I'd thought I'd learned to deal with this.

Sherry had always been independent, and proud of it. But she wasn't selfish. She'd once taken in a friend being abused by a cop husband. She was always first to jump into a homicide case, to do the extra work others hadn't thought of. Before she shared her thoughts on cases with me, even though I wasn't officially a part of the law enforcement family anymore, it was usually the ethical quandaries she wanted to talk about.

Now she would go someplace in silence, in her own thoughts, seeing images only she could watch in her head, to a place that I could only speculate about: Was it anger over the loss of her leg, or a loathing of her own body? Was it self-pity that someone of her character would naturally fight against? A submerged hatred of me, given what my decisions had brought upon her?

I took this new flicker of thought, this idea that she felt a responsibility to reach out to someone else, as a good thing.

While we took a long bend in the trail, I accepted her silence and focused instead on a dark blip in the saw grass ahead. As we got closer, I could make out the green-black body of an alligator halfway out of the lake, up on the shore with its snout up in the air as if it were smelling the breeze. Twenty yards closer, and I could see that it was huge, a fifteen-footer at least. And it had something in its jaws. Twenty more yards, and I could see that wedged in the gator's mouth was a Florida soft-shell turtle, the size of one of those big picnic salad bowls.

"Whoa," I said, and slowed down. The gator concentrated on its catch. Sherry whizzed by on the trail thirty feet away without once turning her head.

I stopped and watched. The gator paid me no mind and continued to work its jaws, applying pressure. I could hear the turtle's shell crackling as the teeth split its plastron: It was still alive, kicking its feet, stretching out its neck in a futile attempt to escape.

3

BILLY MANCHESTER WAS outside—well, his version of outside. He was standing at the railing of the outdoor patio of his penthouse apartment overlooking the island of Palm Beach and the Atlantic beyond. It was the kind of South Florida morning that's lured people to this part of the country for more than a hundred years: sky clear and azure blue, air that's clean and crisp and unsullied by pollution, carrying with it a salt scent of ocean water. The sun warm on the skin, containing an intensity that makes every color pop with a brightness you just don't find in northern climes.

Billy had a folded *Wall Street Journal* in his hand. He was dressed in an immaculately pressed white oxford shirt and tailored trousers despite his stated intention not to visit his law offices today. His nose was in the air, as if scanning the far horizon. And the profile of his coffee-colored skin outlined against the sky gave the impression of some Nubian prince, or at least some *GQ* cover boy.

"I am sometimes astounded by your nearly prescient ability to call on me, Max, just at the simultaneous moment that I am considering calling you," Billy said. "What is it they say about such psychic phenomenon?"

I was still inside his apartment, rooting around in his huge stainless-steel refrigerator, searching for a bottle of Rolling Rock despite the hour and my own stated objective to get back to work. I was dressed in faded jeans and an off-white T-shirt, off-white because of age and a lack of a decent bleaching, not because the color was fashionable. I had on a pair of beat-up deck shoes and no socks. In fact, I had not worn socks since I moved to Florida from Philadelphia some seven years ago.

"Brothers from another mother?" I suggested in response to the question, then opened the beer and walked out to stand with him on the patio.

"That w-wasn't the phrase I was thinking of, Max," he said, his smiling dark eyes now holding mine.

Billy has a profound stutter when he talks with anyone face-to-face. Behind a wall, on a phone, or simply out of sight, his speech is smooth, erudite, and flawless. But put a face in front of him, and a switch turns somewhere in his brain. Notice I do not say he *suffers* from a stuttering problem, because no one who is familiar with Billy and his abilities and success would call him a sufferer or victim.

Billy and I are from the City of Brotherly Love, but the neighborhoods we grew up in were different worlds. I was a third-generation cop from South Philadelphia, a son who was spoon-fed on the ethnic soup of Italians and Poles and Greeks and any other white European immigrant society that could trace its American heritage back to the eighteenth and nineteenth centuries. Yeah, Independence Hall harbored the breakaway English in 1776, but South Philly was home to the stevedores, brick masons, butchers, carpenters, and backbreaking, hard-drinking workers who made the whole new national machine churn.

And yes, Billy's family might well trace its roots back to the slave ships from Africa and the human marketplace where they were sold only a few blocks east and south of where the Liberty Bell once hung. But in our half of the twenty-first century, most blacks had migrated to the north and west sides of the city. And in Billy's neighborhood near Twelfth and Indiana, all the scourges of poverty, drugs, unemployment, and crime were rampant in the 1970s and 1980s. Somehow our mothers met in a church, both of them fleeing religious tradition and abusive husbands. A friendship was born. Billy finally escaped by using his intelligence and drive to get a law degree at Temple University, and a business degree at Wharton. Then he pledged to never live out of the sunshine again.

I fled my own past after my mother found the courage to do away with her husband, my father—our mutual devil. It was Billy's mother who had shown her the way, provided the arsenic, given her the courage. I'd followed the family tradition and become an officer by then. I already knew that my father's abuse was no secret among the fraternity of South Philly cops. The rules of the brotherhood in blue were both a curse and a blessing. No one had intervened during the years of beatings even if they were called to the scene. *Watch out for a brother.* But once it was done, no one let loose the autopsy report that showed the level of poison in my dead father's blood. *Watch out for the family survivors.*

My mother finally succumbed a few years later, comfortable with her oppressor in the grave, and my father's pension—but eaten away by Catholic guilt. I remained a cop until I was shot in the neck during a robbery gone bad. When I took a disability buyout and was determined to leave my past behind, I recalled my mother's urgings to leave the city and look up her North Philly friend's son, the successful lawyer in South Florida. For once, I followed her advice.

Billy had become both my friend and partner. He is the intellectual lawyer with a million contacts, admirers, and grateful clients. I am the headstrong private investigator who despite years of grinding and isolation cannot get the streets, or the work of a beat cop, out of my head.

I tipped my morning beer at Billy and took a long swallow as the sun glinted off the green glass. And my stuttering partner looked out at the gleaming horizon.

"Does that mean you have something for me to do?" I said of his admission that he had been close to calling me before I called him.

"Indeed, M-Max," he said. "There is s-something turned ugly that I b-believe we should p-pursue."

"A WHISTLE-BLOWER?" I said, taking another hit of my beer.

"Yes, wh-whistle-blower."

"So you're doing this thing corporately?" I asked, again trying to get Billy to explain things to me in terms an old street cop could understand.

"Actually it is b-both corporate and governmental. The w-woman works for a private rehabilitation center, b-but wh-what she suspects is that fake orders for wheelchairs and prosthesis are b-being billed to M-Medicare."

"So if it's a government gig with the feds getting ripped off, why doesn't she go to the state attorney's office, or the GAO, or somebody who's actually getting screwed here?" I said.

Billy looked at me. He had already folded the newspaper two more times in his hand. Then he sat down in the patio chair, crossed his legs at the knee, and took on that lawyerly look of his.

"You pay taxes, M-Max. I p-pay taxes. Medicare is funded by us and every other legitimate American," Billy said. "The m-maid, the grocer, the sch-school teacher, the office manager—we are the ones getting ripped off. And if there isn't anything left when we get old and need a wh-wheelchair, we'll b-be the ones hurting."

Though Billy could be ruthlessly efficient in his practice as a financial and corporate consultant, he maintained a true social conscience born of walking the walk as a child of poverty. His own belief that if you made it, you were bound by responsibility to help those trying to do the same, often led him to take on cases that paid nothing—not that he would admit to it.

I was used to his social rhetoric, but he recognized my flinch when he'd used the words *need a wheelchair* and stopped himself.

"I am s-sorry, Max. I did not mean for that to s-sound so p-personal."

It was just the kind of thing Billy would say—an apology for being personal. He's been my best friend for more than eight years. I'd walked into his office unannounced that first time, armed only with a description from my mother, knowing only that his own mother had been an accomplice in the death of my father. For that alone, I owed him a debt.

Without hesitation, he had found me a place to live, a small shack on a river at the edge of the Everglades. It fit my stated needs perfectly. It was isolated, hard to get to, and quiet in a way only nature can be quiet;

a place to grind the rocks in my head, a place to disappear and, yes, a place to hide. Having researched Billy's background, I also entrusted him with my disability insurance payout from the Philadelphia Police Department. He ensured me that he could invest the amount and that I would, given my severely modest plans and lifestyle, never have to work again.

I trusted him, not just because our mothers had trusted each other, despite the differences in their lives, but because I knew the odds he'd beaten, the climb he'd made out of the streets.

Billy had known Sherry for as long as I had. He was the one I'd come to when Sherry was part of a sheriff's team investigating the abduction and killing of children from the suburban communities edging their way out into the once-wild Glades. Because I'd been unlucky enough to discover the body of one child on my river, I had been deemed a suspect. Sherry hadn't trusted me until I ultimately solved that case, rescuing one of the missing children in the process.

Billy had admired Sherry's investigative skills as a detective. And he had seen through her tough-minded way of looking at things without making prejudgments. He had, in fact, realized that before I did. When Sherry and I finally danced around our wariness of each other, and started dating, he'd been deeply pleased. With Billy's wife, an attorney and then a candidate for a federal judgeship, he and Sherry and I were often a social foursome, dining together, or going to some show to which Billy inevitably obtained tickets.

I waved him off his apology for using a reference to wheelchairs and its possible personal connection to Sherry. Her leg fracture and subsequent infection and amputation had occurred while she was officially off-duty. But the fact is that you are always a cop, 24/7. When confronted by a crime, which in our case had been a robbery and abduction leading to multiple shooting deaths in the Glades, she was covered by her sheriff's office insurance. She was taken care of, with her medical bills paid in full by the job. But I had stayed with her, in her Fort Lauderdale house, working, I thought, on the mental rehab I thought she needed.

"Not a problem, Billy. She's actually getting used to it," I said. "You know Sherry, nothing keeps her down."

"B-Bullshit, Max."

You would have to know how infrequently Billy's language goes to the street to realize how strong the statement was. I stared into his face, feeling something rise up into my throat that I have rarely tasted in Billy's presence.

"Sh-She will never g-get used to it, Max. She will adjust. She will f-fight. But you n-never get used to such things."

I cut my eyes away from his, looked out over the lakefront, higher over the barrel tiled roofs of Palm Beach, and even higher to the horizon where the sky touched the ocean.

"OK. When do I meet this whistle-blower?" I asked, and drained the rest of my beer.

4

AT 12:25 P.M., I was sitting in the parking lot of the West Boca Medical Complex waiting for Luz Carmen. Billy had given me the address and the whistle-blower's name. He'd actually made the appointment before I'd arrived at his penthouse, knowing I would accept the assignment, and knowing I would be available for the rest of the day. Within a year of our meeting, I had become Billy's full-time investigator. He had given up going into the streets a long time ago, admitting without chagrin that after what he'd witnessed in his childhood, he would never get his hands dirty again. On the quite literally grimy other hand, I could not stay out of the alleys and shadows and points of danger I'd learned to operate in. Billy and I developed a team, one that often worked well.

I parked two rows back from the entrance to the building, a spread-out affair that looked like they'd borrowed the site plan of the Pentagon but only needed one story. In this part of South Florida—the western cities and suburbs far inland from the ocean—there was no concern for the amount of cheap land developers used. Drain the Everglades by lowering the water table with gouged-out lakes or by dredging funneling canals to the ocean, and then fill and build. It had been going on for a century. Pave paradise, put up a parking lot; apologies to Joni Mitchell.

At 12:30 P.M. exactly, I got a call on my cell. The readout displayed the number Billy had given me.

"Max Freeman," I answered.

"Yes, this is Luz Carmen, may I help you?"

"Uh, you called me, Ms. Carmen."

"Yes, that's possible, sir," said a moderately young woman's voice on the other end of the conversation, if you wanted to call it that. "Yes, sir, I am on my way this very moment, sir."

"Uh, OK, Ms. Carmen, I'm out in the parking lot in a royal blue Ford F-150 pickup truck, two rows back from the sidewalk in the middle," I said, getting the picture. It always makes me shake my head when people hear the title *private investigator* and instantly act like they're in a Jason Bourne spy movie.

Less than two minutes later, I watched a woman whose age matched the telephone voice step outside, sweep the area as if she were worried about being followed, and then make a beeline to my truck.

She was short and slim, maybe five feet two and a hundred pounds. She had long black hair that was either so fine or so meticulously brushed, that even the mild breeze swept it off her shoulders and ruffled it as she approached. She was in heels, skirt just above the knees, and was wearing a white lab coat, like a nurse or doctor.

I started to get out of the truck to greet her when she pierced the windshield with an admonishing look and raised a hand, palm side out. The gesture said: Stay put, please!

Great, I thought—real deep undercover shit, covert ops and everything. I sat still nevertheless while she walked straight to the passenger door, opened it, and climbed in.

"Hi, Ms. Carmen, I assume," I said, giving her my best welcoming and open smile. "I'm Max Freeman, Billy's associate."

"Please drive, Mr. Freeman," she said, staring forward without looking at my face. "We cannot talk here."

Ooooo, secret agent shit. They could be listening in with long-distance audio surveillance equipment. Maybe I ought to get out the special cone of silence. But I said nothing, started the truck, and headed out of the lot. I waited until we were on Glades Road before I asked "Where to, Ms. Carmen?"

"There is a park, Mr. Freeman, up here on the right. We can turn in there and talk where it is safe."

I glanced over at her, already knowing she'd be staring out front, her face stoic and focused. But her fingers were also entwined as they clutched her handbag, her thumb rubbing one knuckle as if there were an itch there that could not be satisfied. She was good at hiding her anxiety, but no one is immune. I decided not to scare her more than she already was and simply followed her directions, letting her feel some control over the situation.

Finally, she directed me into a city park, where I followed a winding ribbon of asphalt to a picnic site. We got out and walked to a wooden table positioned under a huge banyan tree some thirty yards out from the parking area. At mid-afternoon on a fall day with school in session and the workaday tribes at their daily grind, the park was abandoned. Ms. Carmen, I assumed from the lack of a wedding ring, seemed to deem it safe enough and sat on one side of the table as I took the other, looking across, face-to-face, as if we were having some sort of business meeting—which we were, in a way.

"I trust, Mr. Freeman, that Mr. Manchester has filled you in on my situation?" Her language was clean and clipped, the pronunciation of the *r* a touch harder than an Anglo would use. Her English was school-perfect, but it was secondary to her.

"He gave me a very broad outline, Ms. Carmen," I said, copying her tight demeanor. "But I would like to hear it again, in your own words."

Her eyes were dark brown, so dark, in fact, that it was difficult to see the difference between the black pupil and the iris. She stared for an extra second at my face.

"Mr. Manchester says I can trust you."

It was a statement, not a question, so I felt no reason to answer.

She took a deep breath and began.

"I have been working for Mediwheels and Prosthetics for eighteen months, Mr. Freeman. It is the third business I have been with since I obtained my associate nursing degree from Miami Dade Community College," she said, keeping a strict, educated cant to her voice, but not for long.

"I know I need to get my RN degree before I can really work in a hospital, which is what I really want to do. And I know I could just work in one of the nursing homes, which I tried at first. But I really had a hard time with the elderly people and got way too emotional about the problems they were having. I do not like to see their suffering all the time, and . . ."

She caught herself. Recognizing the rambling and the increasingly high pitch of her voice, she stopped, gathered herself, and began again.

"So I took a position with the equipment suppliers instead," she said. "The money is better. You don't see very many patients. It's mostly paper-work. I can save enough to get back into school."

She stopped and looked over at me: I was at a loss.

"That's admirable, Ms. Carmen. You're what, twenty-two? Three?" I said, guessing low, because women like that.

"And you're working toward a better education. That's always a good thing. But please, go on. My understanding is that you've discovered something untoward in the accounting for this business?"

Her hands were back together; the rubbing of the thumb on knuckles had begun yet again.

"It is a small office, Mr. Freeman. There are two treatment rooms stacked only with boxes of forms. There are three wheelchairs, very expensive, top of the line, six-thousand-dollar wheelchairs that are set up for display purposes in the reception area. There are no prosthetics at all—none."

This time when she stopped, I didn't prod. I was thinking instead of the wheelchair that Sherry owned, and the busy, equipment-filled therapy rooms at Broward General Hospital where she did her rehabili-tation. Sherry was already talking about the possibility of a prosthetic that could replace her lower leg and allow her to run, like some guy trying to get into the Olympics with a thing that looks like a fiberglass spatula attached to his partially missing leg.

"They are stealing," Carmen said with enough force to snap me back to attention. "They are stealing the Medicare and Medicaid numbers of patients and using them to order expensive wheelchairs and medical equipment, and then cashing in the reimbursements themselves."

Again I didn't prod; I just rolled the scenario around in my head. Money from government programs meant to help disabled people was being funneled into the hands of con men who figured out how to game the system—nothing new. When I was a cop in Philadelphia, it was the food stamps, bartered on the streets like Monopoly money, traded for drugs and booze like any stolen merchandise. Go up the line, and subsidized housing gets used the same way. Hell, some big-name congressman in New York just got popped for using a rent-subsidized apartment as his elections office. I could now see why Billy got into this. This kind of thing enrages him: I, on the other hand . . .

"So does this illegal transaction of phony requests and exchange of funds take place in your office, Ms. Carmen?" I finally said.

"No, they wouldn't do it there. No, someone gathers the numbers and then delivers them."

"And do you know where this place is—the drop-off?"

"No," she said, and turned her face away.

Ms. Carmen did not lie easily or well. There was something there that I needed to read. The sense of indignation was missing. This wasn't just some employee angered by the unfairness of it all. I've seen the disgust of people in North Philadelphia when the drug dealing got so bad that their kids couldn't safely walk to school, or had to stay inside on summer evenings for fear of getting shot in some 9 mm pissing match over a corner.

This woman was scared in a personal way: Was this an admission of her own guilt?

"So who is actually siphoning off the numbers?" I said. "Who makes the delivery?"

"A few months ago, I got my brother a job there," she said, keeping her eyes down. "I was trying to help him. He has not done well for himself these past few years. After I vouched for him, he promised he would work hard, and do what he was told, and always be on time."

Now her confident voice lost its power and conviction. A tear formed at the corner of one eye, but was held there as if by will alone; it did not drop. She blinked.

"So your brother is the one delivering the numbers?" I said, stating what she could not.

"His name is Andrés, Andrés Carmen. And he does not have good friends, Mr. Freeman. I am afraid for both him and myself."

Nothing new here, I thought. Same game with a different name: numbers running, working the outlets, gathering the tickets, hoofing them to a place where they are sorted and used. Can you say Italian lottery, or the numbers game? *Bolita?*

If I am surprised at all, it's because in this day of electronic communication, instant messaging, and email at the press of a finger, this kind of enterprise wouldn't usually be employing a hand-delivery system. It made me think of old-school criminals doing something new that they weren't quite used to, so they stick to the tried and true.

"Your brother makes these deliveries when, at the end of the day? Twice a week?"

"Only once a week, on Fridays, I think," Carmen said.

"And does he go straight there after leaving your office?"

"I don't know. I tried to follow him once, but I couldn't keep up."

"OK. What does your brother look like? How can I recognize him?"

Now she hesitated. This had gone beyond making a whistle-blower complaint, and had taken on the feeling of a personal betrayal. This was where it always got them: a mother turning in a son's drug use, a daughter confessing her father's sexual abuse.

I'd seen it a dozen times in my own home, tucked in a space at the top of the stairs when my father's own friends, the blue brotherhood, would show up in uniform to answer a complaint from one of the neighbors. They'd always take my father outside first. Then a uniform would stand in the kitchen with my bruised and tearful mother.

"This is the third complaint this year, Mrs. Freeman. Is he hitting you?"

My mother knew that if she answered, her husband could lose his job. She knew her son would lose his father. She knew it would be the end of a family, the loss of a confidant, a shoulder, even if the shoulder was sometimes hard and often brutal. I never heard my mother answer. And the uniformed cop would never ask twice.

"Please don't let him get hurt, Mr. Freeman," Carmen said, looking into my eyes. Her strong will couldn't hold the tear drop this time.

I stayed silent, waiting.

"My height, my coloring," she finally said. "He wears a Marlins baseball cap, turned backward. You know how they do. And he is driving an old Toyota, dusty white you know, from the sun."

"And how old is he?"

"He is nineteen years old."

"So he's not a juvenile." It was a statement, not a question.

"His date of birth is June fourteenth, nineteen-ninety," she said looking hard into my eyes.

"You know Mr. Manchester is a lawyer?"

"Yes."

"We'll look up your brother's juvenile record."

"And you will find it," she said, losing a bit of the bravado now. "I am very much trying to save him, Mr. Freeman."

She was back to staring at her fingers, the rubbing more severe now. And for some reason, I was thinking about the callus she'd built up on that fine delicate knuckle of hers. I was trying to think of something to say to assure her that things will be all right, when I knew they wouldn't. And while both of us were avoiding eye contact, I began to hear the thrumming of an electronic heartbeat pulsing somewhere in the distance, and growing.

When I looked up out from the shade of the tree, I saw a metallic green Chevrolet Monte Carlo swinging through the parking lot, its chrome wheels spinning the sunlight. The windows were illegal black. The driver didn't seem to be in a hurry. At first, I thought it was "just kids." But when I turned and looked back at Carmen, she was knitting her brow.

"It's OK, Ms. Carmen," I said.

But she was looking past my shoulder to the approaching car.

Then I heard the bass pounding of the music suddenly go louder, as if a barrier had been lowered. When I glanced back, a rear window was rolling down.

Bap, bap, bap.

It wasn't until the third round that I launched myself over the top of the picnic table and swept Luz Carmen off the bench with a flying tackle. I could hear the bullets in the tree leaves above us making the sound of ripping cloth.

Bap, bap, baaaaaaap.

Fucking automatic, I registered in my head. When I looked through the legs of the picnic table, I could see the muzzle flash coming out of the Monte Carlo's back window just as the driver punched it and sent the ass end of the car slewing to the right. The scream of the friction between hot rubber and asphalt added a whining alto to the bass line. In seconds, they were gone.

Now it was stone quiet—amplified silence after chaos. I rolled off Luz Carmen, whose entire body was trembling. I scanned her for any sign that she was hit. When I got to her eyes, they were wide and locked on something in the distance, instead of squeezed shut like most people's eyes would be under the circumstances.

"You OK?" I said.

No reaction. I pushed up to my knees. "Ms. Carmen, are you all right?"

She was still wide-eyed and stiff.

"Ms. Carmen," I said, not sure why I was asking a question of someone in shock. "Please don't tell me that was your brother."

5

"Jesus, Max."

As I said, Billy is not often taken to swearing. So when he starts out that way, it's a warning that you've probably crossed one of his lines, and he is not pleased.

"Your new client can be very convincing," I said, trying that tactic where you bring in the fact that your boss was the one who sent you out there to begin with, hoping you might spread the blame.

"Max, you left the scene of a crime."

"Well, technically, yes."

"Well, technically it was an assault with a deadly weapon. Nontechnically, it was a drive-by shooting, during which you were able to identify the car involved—and if I know you, the caliber of the gun, and possibly the license plate number."

"No. They were smart enough to remove that ahead of time," I said, realizing that I was getting defensive now. I knew that any good law enforcement agency in the area would have a pretty good file on a metallic green, jacked-up Monte Carlo with blacked-out windows, even with no numbers.

"No one was injured, Billy," I repeated. "Once your Ms. Carmen was calm, she was adamant that we return to her office. She said if she came in late after lunch it would only raise suspicions among her bosses. She said she didn't want to break any of her normal routine, because all eyes were going to be on her if you should get someone from the feds to raid the place."

I took a long breath, listening to silence on the other end of the cell phone.

"See," I finally said. "She's pretty damned convincing."

"So you're in the parking lot now?" Billy said, moving past it, like the good lawyer he is. What's done is done; you move on and tackle the problems that you can.

"Yeah," I said. "She said she always leaves work at five fifteen. I'm going to follow her home, just to make sure."

I figured that the least I could do was keep an eye out for the woman, even if our little lunchtime surprise was just a carload of idiot punks getting a kick out of scaring people in the park. Of course, I didn't believe that. Coincidence is crap in this business. And besides, since leaving the Philadelphia Police Department after getting shot, I'd had the luxury of time. I also had an off-the-clock burden of responsibility.

If something happened to Ms. Carmen after I blew off the incident as an urban prank, wrote up a report, and forgot it after shift change, I'd be right back where I'd often been as a cop: cynical, depressed, and complicit.

"OK, Max," Billy said, perhaps forgiving. "That sounds prudent."

Prudent started with a *pr* that would have taken him three attempts to get off his tongue if we'd been speaking face-to-face.

"What can you give me over the phone?"

I told him about Ms. Carmen's brother, gave him the name and the DOB, knowing he'd be punching the information into one of his array of computer databases as we spoke.

"All right, Max, that's a start. I'll work on this and review it with you later," Billy said. As a bit of a techno-wizard, he didn't even like using cell phones to discuss business. Anyone with money could put together the kind of listening devices and triangulation tracking governments use surreptitiously these days. Billy is no Big Brother phobe, but you only have to read the newspaper to know the capabilities of these systems. And as every law enforcement officer in the world knows, if we have the equipment, the bad guys are usually a step ahead of us.

After hanging up with Billy, I sat. Surveillance is the armpit duty of every private investigator, police detective, security officer, tinker, tailor, spy who ever worked it. You sit and turn your head on a swivel, running through the checklist, thinking about possibilities and scenarios for as long as you can stand it—about fifteen minutes. Then you get bored as hell and fight to stay awake.

A former Philly partner of mine didn't even pretend. He'd straight-away start snoring, with his wristwatch alarm set to go off every thirty minutes his only show of loyalty to the job. Another acquaintance, a Florida Department of Law Enforcement agent, busied himself writing novels while he was on watch. After an hour's time sitting in the South Florida heat at midday, I moved my truck. I'd been eyeballing the only spot of shade in the lot while people, some obviously medical personnel, others looking like everyday patients, came and went. When the shady spot opened up, I stole it.

With my windows rolled down and a blessed breeze flowing through, it was tolerable as I ran the shooting through my head for the umpteenth time. Metallic green ghetto car—obviously amateurs to be driving such a recognizable and easily tracked auto. Loud bass music: So they were also not concerned with anyone hearing them coming.

I closed my eyes and tried to do a bit of relaxation therapy and self-hypnosis: The darkened back window rolls down and the muzzle of what, a rifle, at least eight inches of barrel, a V-site on the front, the well-machined *bap, bap, bap* of semiauto; and then the *baaaaaaap* of full auto ripping the tree leaves.

I opened my eyes. The shitheads inside the car might have been sim-pleminded gangbangers, but the weapon was not. It wasn't some cheap TEC-9 or Lorcin pistol they could buy for 150 bucks on the street. It was a hell of a lot more sophisticated, an MP5-style rifle and a hell of a lot more accurate. So how had they missed?

An incompetent shooter would usually start firing low; the recoil might jerk his aim up into the trees. But this guy started high, and stayed there. Also, what was with changing the semiauto rounds to a full spray? Yeah, it's just the flick of a switch on a quality weapon—but why?

Maximum fear factor? Had the whole thing been a warning, the shooter spraying the trees above our heads to show how easily it could be done? Christ knows, I'd done enough in my past to piss people off. In my last assignment, everyone but Sherry and I died. And I hadn't put myself in the sights of any drug dealers since I'd moved to Florida. That, of course, left Ms. Carmen and her still-mysterious brother. But as far as I knew, white-collar Medicare criminals weren't blowing away informants, or one another, in the streets yet.

Still, there was that coincidence thing. I blinked my eyes fully awake, swiveled my head again, went through the list, and then checked my watch. If she was as anal as I thought, Ms. Carmen would be out of work in two more hours. I would follow her home. I'd check around back to make sure there wasn't an alley or a maintenance lane behind her townhouse. I'd sit in my truck and watch until dark, and then sit for an hour longer. Then I'd talk myself into leaving, figuring that if the shooters in the metallic green Monte Carlo were only trying to scare her, they, or whoever paid them to do their little gunplay act, would wait until tomorrow to see if she'd cower.

At 7:30 P.M., I called Billy.

"I'm going home," I said. "She seems to be safe inside."

"Good," he said.

"Find anything on the brother?"

"Lots of minor drug arrests. Delivery and so forth—minor stuff if you're a teenager living along Tamarind Avenue in West Palm."

"But enough to make connections with a variety of buyers and sellers," I said.

"True enough. Let's talk about it tomorrow," Billy said. "No doubt you're due at Sherry's."

"Yeah," I said, but then worried about the lack of enthusiasm in my voice.

"Go see your girl, Max," Billy said.

"Good night, Billy."

IT WAS LATE when I got to Sherry's. Light from a half-moon was filtering down through the big oak trees spread throughout her neighborhood. Years before the residential boom in downtown Fort Lauderdale, this had been a quiet collection of 1950s bungalows called Victoria Park. When she bought the house, Sherry used her status as a deputy for the Broward Sheriff's Office and worked the real estate agent until she got him below eighty thousand dollars.

"The last house east of Federal Highway that's ever going to go for under a hundred," she liked to quote the guy as saying. That was in the late 1980s. The going price went to six times that in the crazy postmillennial years. Now it was sinking back to where it always should have been, and marketing mouths were going back to pass the area off as "historical."

I had to admit, if large trees with hanging moss, heavily laden trellises of bougainvillea and plumbago, and minimal street lighting meant historic, then so be it. I liked it because most of the time it was quiet.

I parked my truck at the end of the driveway and walked up past Sherry's MG convertible, shrouded with a canvas covering since our ill-fated Everglades trip.

I bypassed the wooden ramp I'd built to the front door before Sherry was released from the hospital and went on through a gate to the enclosed backyard. I knew she'd be in her refuge. As I closed the gate behind me, I could hear the hum of the water circulators, and the slight *splash-kick-splash* of her relentless, rhythmic swimming stroke.

I stepped up onto the wooden deck and tossed my backpack into the empty rope hammock. The house was dark save for a small kitchen light we always left on. Out here, there was only the glow of the pool lights, a cast of aqua blue that shimmered up into the oak tree above and played in the leaves there, dappling and flickering with soft color, creating an opposite feeling to what was going on in the water.

There Sherry was working. After her amputation, she had decided to install a current system at one end of her backyard pool. With the flick of a switch, a series of jet sprays kicked in and shot a steady stream of water in one direction just below the surface. The setup required a big pump for recirculation but effectively created a current Sherry could swim against, stroking at her steady pace for as long as electricity held out. Sometimes I wondered which would give out first.

I stood with my hands in my pockets, watching. While the pool lights gave the world up here an ethereal look, below it had a paling effect. From here, Sherry's long, single slender leg appeared as a bloodless white color as she kicked, moving with the constant rhythm of a double thunk—*flump, flump, flump-flump*—like a heartbeat. The crisp movement caused the water around her foot to cleave and then fold in on itself to create a hollow sound. I watched for a full five minutes, and her rhythm never faltered.

If she could see me through her tinted goggles, she didn't stop to acknowledge me. Maybe her eyes were closed in concentration, I thought; maybe she didn't give a damn. I turned and walked inside the house.

I didn't turn the lights on, negotiating only by the stove's overhead. I took two bottles of Rolling Rock from the refrigerator door and then stood at the sink, looking out the window at the rippling aqua glow while I drank the first beer with three long pulls. The coldness gave me a small brain freeze, and when I squeezed my eyes shut, I could feel tears at their edges. I rinsed the empty, dropped it into the recycling bin, and went back outside.

Sitting in one of the patio chairs, I took off my shoes, rolled up my pant legs, and opened the second beer. I took a smaller sip this time and then sat for a bit, watching Sherry's movements, the turn of her head, always breathing on the left side, not alternating like they teach you, her hands coming up out of the water, each stroke ending with a flip of the wrist: Reach out, pull through, kick out at the end, her rhythm like a metronome. And always the *flump-flump* of that single foot.

There was no telling when she was going to stop. Sometimes she'd be at it for an hour, sometimes two. I told myself it didn't bother me, and then moved down to the pool corner to sit on the steps. I sat on the edge, with my feet and calves submerged, and sipped the beer. I waited as I watched her head, her usual sunlight blonde hair darkened by the water.

I knew what she was doing; I'd done the same thing myself when I came to Florida to get away from the streets of Philadelphia. Descended from a long line of policemen, I thought of the job as a duty, a lifelong commitment. Then one night, while responding to a store's silent alarm, I came face-to-face with an armed robber. He got off the first round, his bullet piercing my neck.

In reaction, I returned fire. But in my hesitation and piss-poor aim, I hit the second person coming out of the store, a thirteen-year-old accomplice who took my 9-mm slug in the back as he twisted away. The round severed his spinal cord, and he was dead before his body touched concrete. I left my career in the street, blood pooling under the body of a teenager.

After Billy set me up in the research shack on the river, nearly every night there I'd paddle my canoe upstream into the Glades, keeping that rhythm, punishing myself, looking for some kind of solace. I knew Sherry was doing the same thing now, and I knew the answer wasn't there.

For several years, I'd kept up a habit of touching the spot on my neck where the robber had shot me. Unconsciously, my fingertips would go to the smooth, circular scar tissue and caress it. A while after I met Sherry, I quit the habit. Her love had helped me move on. I wanted to do the same for her.

Staring down at my feet in the water, I was about to stand when the *flump-flump* stopped. By the time I looked up, she'd dipped her head under the water and executed a powerful breaststroke to move out of the current and over to my side. When her face surfaced, she was smiling and breathing hard—happy to see me.

"Well, hello there," she said in between deep gulps of breath. "How long have you been watching?"

She was still floating, her chin just above the surface, those malleable blue-green eyes of hers taking on the color of the water, with the azure tint that always seemed to assert itself when she was in a good mood.

I took a quick glance at my half-empty bottle and wagged it a bit.

"Long enough for a couple," I said.

She took another stroke closer and half stood, putting her wet hands on my knees, and then pushed herself up with her arms, as if she were doing one of her impressive workout dips. Then she raised herself until her face was level with mine.

"So, were you assessing my stroke, or what?" she said, her breathing starting to subside.

"Pretty proficient," I said, setting the bottle on the tile behind me without taking my eyes off hers.

She pushed herself higher and closer. I could feel the water dampening my pants legs and dripping onto my shirt. She moved her lips onto mine and slightly opened her mouth; her breath was warm.

When she broke off the kiss, we held eye contact. And I knew the question on her face was a reflection of the question on mine: Do you really want to do this?

She answered it first. "Come on in," she said, backing away with a teasing smile. "The water's fine."

I undid the first button on my shirt and then gave up and pulled it over my head. My khakis came off with some effort, and I stepped down into the pool, the warm water sliding up my rib cage until I was nose-to-nose with Sherry. She kissed me again.

With a nervous flutter in my chest—Was I fifteen again?—I asked myself: What do I do? Where do I go? How careful? How much?

I touched her shoulders with my palms to shape the muscle there, and then let them slide to her back. She had a swimmer's body, defined and hard. I pressed my fingertips into the muscle fibers and massaged them. She broke off the kiss with a shiver, hooked her thumbs under the shoulder straps of her suit, and slipped it down.

Only then did I pull her to me, chest to chest, my nose in her hair, which had not lost the smell of her perfume, despite the chlorine. She nuzzled the side of my neck, and I let my hands flow over the curve of her hips. I was on my toes, partially floating, my knees flexed to match her height, forming a natural lap. I started to draw her onto me, holding the backs of her thighs—in that aching zone of passion, hunger, past my tentative beginnings. As I used my strength to pull her onto me, and my hand slid down her left thigh, it lost purchase at the point where that limb ended.

I fumbled. She jerked at the touch of my palm across the flap of her amputation. I tried to recover, reaching again to hold her close, but she twisted and then pushed away like a young girl who's realized she's gone too far in her foreplay. I hesitated, and did not try to stop her from leaving.

6

AFTER MY HAND touched the skin flap of Sherry's amputation, she'd quickly pulled up her suit and stroked over to the steps. On one leg, she hopped up and out of the water and grabbed a nearby towel, slung it around her waist, and made her way inside. I stayed in the water, rested the back of my head on the gutter, and closed my eyes, listening to the sound of night insects, taking in the odor of night-blooming jasmine.

Later I sat at the kitchen counter, drinking beer in the dark, feeling sorry for myself. There were techniques I'd taught myself to control my anger when I worked on the streets of Philadelphia as a foot patrolman: when a punk-assed kid mouthed off when I asked him not to loiter in front of the bistro on South Street, or when some dealer was lucky enough not to be carrying when I finally thought I'd outsmarted him and he just smirked and turned out his empty pockets.

Grain of sand, I'd tell myself, let it go. Form that omega sign with your ring finger and thumb, a reminder not to let the anger rule you. Get the small rubber pinkie ball out of your pocket and squeeze it in your palm—a hundred times, no, two hundred. I'm not sure any of them worked then; I wasn't sure they'd do tonight.

I'd made love to Sherry hundreds of times, many of them joyful moments in that very pool. But I'd never made love to one-legged Sherry. It had been nearly a year; no matter how understanding I tried to be, knowing my needs were no match for what she was enduring, I was still failing. You're insensitive, Max. You're thinking with your dick, Max. Don't be a Neanderthal, Max. Finally, I poured half the beer out in the sink and rinsed it. The third bottle of the night wasn't helping; a fourth or fifth wouldn't, either.

When I went to her room, the lights were still on. She was sitting up in bed, dressed now in one of my big Temple Owls T-shirts and a pair of sweatpants. She was on her side of the bed, the same side she'd had since our relationship started. But a long rectangular mirror was propped lengthwise against her inside hip and extended to the foot of the bed. From my viewpoint, it was a four-foot, framed length of particle board. The mirrored side faced her.

"Hurting?" I asked, already knowing the answer.

"Yeah, a little bit," she said without looking up. Her head was cocked to the side so she could stare into the mirror.

Within the first couple of months of her amputation, Sherry had developed a pain in her leg, the missing one. She began complaining that the missing leg was in such pain she couldn't stand it. This is a woman with a pain threshold higher than anyone I've ever met. When I dragged her through the Everglades with a compound fracture, she'd refused to cry out. So my layman's logic asked: How could something that's not there anymore hurt? But I also knew that she was suffering.

The pain was in her brain, as it is in everyone's, her doctors told her. Pain is a perceived thing. They explained cortical perception and told her she would have to change the feeling that it manifests. Sherry was skeptical. Hell, I was completely unbelieving. But after a series of different techniques, Sherry's therapists found that mirror-imaging treatment worked for her. By positioning the long mirror beside her, she could see the reflected image of her healthy leg, lying right there, a replacement, at least in her brain, for the missing limb. Using this, the pain subsided.

I stripped off my clothes, put on a pair of workout shorts, and climbed into my side of the bed. I had always slept naked in the past. Sherry dimmed the lights but did not turn them off. I rolled onto my left shoulder, facing the opposite way, knowing she might spend hours gazing at the faux image of herself.

Finally, she reached out and laid her fingers lightly on my head.

"I'm sorry, Max."

"It's OK, baby," I said, lying again.

"I thought I was ready," she said. "I was trying."

"I know, baby. It's OK."

The lying came off my tongue with such simplicity, with such martyrdom. I rolled over onto my back and took her hand in mine, interlacing our fingers.

"It's going to take time," she said.

"I know," I said, and this time it was the truth. But the next lie came quickly, too. "I didn't mean to pressure you."

When I looked at her face, the familiar line of her nose and slant of her jaw, the way her blonde hair fell across her cheek, I also saw the framed piece of particle board, the barrier between us.

"Are you working for Billy tomorrow?" she said.

"No. Not till Friday."

"Will you come with me to meet this guy at the gym?"

"Which guy?"

"The one I was telling you about—the deputy from the hit-and-run."

It is unusual for her to ask me along. In the past, we'd worked some cases together because the circumstances demanded it. But Sherry is the kind of detective who likes her independence, even when carrying out quasi-official duties.

"OK, sure," I said. "If you don't think I'll be in the way."

She squeezed my hand and grinned. "Just stay in the background. And don't knock anything over."

I smiled back, right before she moved her eyes to the mirror again. I stared up at the ceiling, and at some point rolled back onto my shoulder.

A bond between us is fraying, I thought, but we are both trying not to let the fibers go loose.

AT 11:00 THE next morning, I loaded Sherry's wheelchair into the bed of my truck and we took a drive up to A1A in Fort Lauderdale. I had the windows down, which I try to do whenever the temperature falls below eighty degrees. Out at my river shack at the edge of the Everglades, it never gets as hot as it does in the city. Out there, I am constantly shaded by towering water oaks and cypress trees that are hundreds of years old. And my shack sits up on stilts that are speared down into waist-deep water. You cannot get to my place without a canoe or flat-bottomed boat. The shade and the water eliminate two of the heat sources that plague South Florida: dominating sunshine and thermal-absorbing concrete. An eighty-five-degree day in downtown West Palm Beach or Miami is a seventy-five-degree one at my shady spot on the river.

What I don't have out there is the ocean breeze and the smell of fresh salt air. When we hit A1A at the Las Olas Boulevard intersection, I took a deep and appreciative lungful and looked out over the vast blueness of the ocean. I thought, If I could move my shade trees and my cool river water to the shore, I might live here forever. But the only way to do that would be to eliminate 120 years of urban development. Forget it, Max; this isn't the Florida of the 1890s.

When the driver behind me blew his horn, I realized I'd been sitting at a green light and moved on. A few blocks later, Sherry directed me to turn into a city parking lot. While I unloaded her chair, I surveyed the area. There was some sort of high-rise construction site to the south, the International Hall of Fame Pool behind us to the west, and an older, 1970s-style retail complex to the north. The north building was a two-story sun-washed stucco box. The first floor featured a liquor store, a sandwich shop, and a beachwear boutique. Upstairs was a place called the Iron Pump, which had a neon sign and floor-to-ceiling windows.

I already doubted that there would be an elevator in the place as Sherry climbed out of the truck and into her wheelchair. But as we approached the entrance to the building, we got a heads-up from a skinny guy sitting on a stool just inside the shade. When he nodded, the cigarette in the corner of his mouth nodded with him.

"You goin' upstairs, they's a freight elevator in the back there," he said, hooking his thumb down the hall. The man's arms were covered in tattoos from his wrists to his bony shoulders, and he was holding a small miniature poodle in his lap. His eyes were as yellow as the dog's.

Though both Sherry and I were casually dressed in shorts and shirts, they weren't the kind that would indicate we were going for a workout. Our natural cop wariness must have shown.

"They's another chair dude up there now," the man said, again with the nod. "Tol' me to give y'all directions."

"Thanks," I said, matching his head movement, minus the cigarette.

The freight elevator was clunky and smelled of stale booze and sweat, which only served as a hint of odors to come. Sherry was silent. I knew she was anticipating the scene, steeling herself for the introduction to come, working out a dialogue ahead of time. I had already decided to make myself as unassuming as possible.

When we got off the freight elevator, we entered a corridor open to the outside at either end. Along the hallway, there were two doors to the east, two to the west. On the west side, I could hear music. And it took a couple of measures before I tagged it as "Hell Patrol" by Judas Priest. I was guessing that if I put my fingertips on the cinderblock wall next to me, I would feel the bass vibration. But given the looks of the flaked and mildewed paint job, I kept my hands in my pockets.

Sherry rolled down to a glass door and started to open it herself before I could get there; so I stood back after grabbing the handle to hold it. Anyone inside would see her glide in unassisted, with me following.

Inside the music wasn't as loud as I'd anticipated, and the clanking of metal was off the beat. There was one big room before us, spread out and planted with chromed-up exercise stations, as in some metallic cyber garden: iron stalks of pipes and steel cable, stacks of heavy black plates, and small cushioned red pads attached at seemingly impromptu places. The odor was of stale sweat and close heat and ripe testosterone.

Sunlight was pouring through the windows onto a row of treadmills and stationary bicycles. But at mid-morning, there was only one person jogging there with his iPod strapped to his arm. I spotted an office cubicle carved out with a half wall of fabric at the far front corner. But the action was obviously in the back, where I could see the free weight stacks flanking the bench press and squatting rack, where eight big guys were milling in front of the wall of mirrors, looking at themselves. A couple of others were spotting for a man pumping a load on the bench press, his high-pitched hissing cutting through the music. No one looked directly our way, but I got that same feeling I did when entering a neighborhood bar where I was new: No one missed the entrance of strangers.

While I was still taking in the scene, Sherry rolled off toward the back corner. She had spotted her appointment, a guy in a sleeveless sweatshirt with bulky shoulders and no legs. He was sitting in a wheelchair and pumping a set of iron dumbbells with both arms. When we approached, I saw that his eyes were closed. Despite the fact that he was facing a wall of mirrors, he was not looking at his image. Sherry stopped a few feet away.

"Marty Booker?" she said in greeting.

The man did not stop his methodical curling; left, right, left, right. His biceps were bulging with the effort, blood pumping through engorged veins that looked like fat blue worms crawling just under the skin. He also did not open his eyes.

"How'd you guess, Detective?" he said, the words leaking out between clenched teeth.

"Familiar hair color," Sherry said.

There was a twitch of a smile at the corner of the guy's mouth as he tightened his lips to finish the repetitions, and then dropped the weights to the floor beside him. Booker took a towel that was draped across one of his wheels and wiped his hands. He finally looked Sherry in the eye and offered his hand, which she shook, and then nodded up at me.

"This is my friend Max Freeman."

The man's handshake was hard, the skin almost hot to the touch. I could feel the callus on his inside palm. He looked me in the face.

"You're the dude who helped out with the junk man a few years back, right? The serial killer doing druggies in the northwest."

"It was Sherry's case," I said.

"Yeah," he said, turning a smile back at Sherry. "She blew the guy's face off, if I remember."

It was, in fact, a case I'd been pulled into by Billy. One result was that I had surprised the serial killer in his own lair only to have him get the drop on me. He was about to finish me off when Sherry saved my ass by putting a 9 mm into the man's brain.

Sherry said nothing, and kept any recognition of the incident from showing in her eyes. Instead, she looked down at Booker's wheelchair.

"Nice rig," she said.

"Yeah," Booker said, thumping the wheels with the heels of his hand. "Nothing but the best for a gimped-up cop; your county tax dollars at work."

But he quickly dumped the cynical tone and returned Sherry's attempt to break the ice by assessing her own chair.

"Yours ain't bad, either. Built for speed, eh?"

"Yeah," Sherry said. "Lightweight alloy, it's good for distances."

Booker nodded and looked down in his lap. "Never was one for the long run. More of a short blast kinda' guy."

Sherry was silent, seemingly lost for words, an unusual predicament for her. I was starting to feel an uneasy creaking in my knees, like I needed to move and get out of the way. But then I sensed the movement of others in the room as a couple of the corner lifters inched their way over to us.

"And hell, now he's an even shorter blast," said a voice from the group, a comical tone in his voice. "Just kidding . . ."

Sherry pulled one wheel back, spinning her chair around.

"Well, it's you, Detective Sergeant Richards," said a mutt-faced man dressed in a black stretch-fabric shirt, hemmed above the shoulders to show his bulky biceps, and tight at the waist. His matching black shorts were as loose as the shirt was tight, hanging down below his knees. He had one of those half-smiling faces on that tries to show he's being friendly and funny, but smart-assed and dangerous at the same time. It probably worked on teenage girls looking for adventure. It only made me begin flexing and curling my fingers.

"Never seen you in here before, Detective," the man said with one of those glances back at his friends, to indicate he was speaking for all them. "Trying to get back in shape, ma'am?"

Sherry cut a look at Booker to assess his reaction. I figured she was looking for something that might indicate friends or foes. When she got no sign, she turned back to mutt-face.

"Did someone invite you over here, McKenzie?" she said to the guy. "Because we're having a conversation that entails stringing nouns, verbs, and adjectives together, so I doubt that you have the capacity to participate."

I heard a couple of sniggers escape from someone's mouth. Sherry was still staring at mutt-face, a.k.a. McKenzie, who, I'd guessed by now, was some sort of cop. Despite being verbally dinged in front of his buds, he kept the faked-up smile on his face in place.

"Hey, you're a stitch, Detective," he said, gesturing to Sherry's missing leg, "pardon the pun. But we were just wondering if maybe you were recruiting for some special unit with our buddy Booker here—a new gimp patrol or something."

I did not move. I'm about six feet three and a lean and ambling 215 pounds. I'm quicker than I look, and I knew my stamina was twice as good as anyone in the room other than Sherry. She on the other hand is as lean as a cheetah. Everyone here outmuscled us in bulk. It would be nasty if we had to get into it. But I'd learned over the years to let Sherry handle her own situations. To interfere is to hint that she can't take care of herself, and that's the last thing anyone in their right mind would want to do with Sherry.

She just nodded at the gimp patrol comment and then gestured to McKenzie's crotch, matching his cynical smile.

"Why, McKenzie?" she said. "You have a recent amputation or something? You are looking a little light these days."

Now the sniggers turned to laughter, peppered with a few *woofs*.

"Smart mouth for a girl in a wheelchair," McKenzie said.

I could see him flex the muscle in his abnormal-size neck, giving Sherry that shrug they must learn when they're posing in front of the mirror. It's not much different behavior from that of a cane toad that puffs itself up to appear bigger, in order to scare off an attacker.

McKenzie was sizing me up. I had several inches on him, but we were probably the same weight. I'd have him on reach if it got physical, but you'd have to be careful not to let him get a hold of you.

"Don't look at him, dickless," Sherry said, careful not to let anger seep into her voice, thereby letting the scenario spin out as locker room jibbing. "Challenge me, tough guy." She waved her hand around the room, indicating the variety of workout machines.

"Let's see if you can make my short list," she said, looking him up and down. "Excuse the pun."

McKenzie huffed and looked back at his buddies. And when no help was offered, he turned around to Sherry. "You choose, little girl," he said.

Sherry looked around like she was deciding, but I knew exactly where she was going.

"Dips, rockhead," she said, pointing at two matching iron towers that included pronged handles at about chest height. She wheeled over and McKenzie and his gang followed. When she unbuttoned her blouse and pulled it off to reveal a workout bra underneath, I instantly wondered if she'd had this scenario in mind all along. Her arms and shoulders rippled with finely cut muscles, slim and corded, devoid of any softness that might indicate fat of any kind.

McKenzie stepped up and peeled off his shirt to go naked from the waist. He flexed his pectorals, which jumped like trained gerbils on his chest, and then tried to stretch his huge biceps, which because of their size seemed to bend his arms at a permanent angle.

An older man in khakis and a polo shirt with the gym's logo stitched on the breast appeared from behind the half-wall office and sauntered over. When he caught my eye and recognized me as a stranger, I gave him a shrug, as if I had no idea what was going on. He stood next to me and folded his arms, watching.

After locking the wheels on her chair, Sherry pushed herself to a standing position. On one leg, she hopped over to the machine on the right and positioned herself between the handles that flanked her shoulders. She put her palms on the two grips, with her elbows cocked behind her shoulders. The fabric of her bra stretched tight across her breasts. McKenzie followed suit on the machine next to her, his smile intact.

"Count out your own reps, McKenzie," Sherry said. "Unless you need help from your boys here if you get past ten."

She took a small hop and pressed herself up into a locked elbow position, and then lowered herself to the start. Then she pressed her entire body weight up again. McKenzie jumped up on his tower to match her.

"One, two, three . . ."

The music in the place had changed over to "Down 'n' Dirty" by Steelheart. I took the gym manager by the elbow and urged him toward his office.

"Maybe you could show me what kind of contract you have for a membership," I said.

7

I KNEW THE outcome of Sherry's little "challenge" without watching or listening. But the manager couldn't keep himself from peering around the corner of his cubicle for the first sixty seconds of our impromptu meeting.

Sherry has been doing those dips ever since I've known her. She's been knocking them out on the curved stainless handles of the ladder into her pool for years. Even back then, she could do thirty reps without breathing hard. After her amputation, and the consequent loss of 20 percent of her body weight, I'd seen her do fifty before giving up, seemingly out of boredom. Mutt-faced McKenzie had maxed out at twenty-three. He was, of course, pressing an enormous muscle mass, which weighs even more than fat.

After Sherry had kicked his ass in front of his other lifter friends, she invited Booker to lunch quietly. I thanked the gym manager for a brochure and followed them out, depositing the printed materials in a trash can outside. On the sidewalk, Sherry and Booker wheeled over to a café on A1A. But I begged off, opting to go sit on the beachfront retaining wall with my feet in the sand and watch a trio of kite surfers fly off the waves and swells of the ocean in the shimmering sunlight.

Less than an hour later, I heard Sherry's wheels crunching on the sandy sidewalk behind me. I let her pull up beside me, without turning. She said nothing, and I hoped she was enjoying the same sight I was. She knew, of course, that I was aware of her presence. It's a gift that couples gain over time.

Finally, she broke the silence.

"Want to go swimming?"

When I turned to see if she was serious, the mischievous smile on her face answered the question. Then she stood up, put her palms on the three-foot-tall wall, and swung her torso and leg over it like a gymnast on a pommel horse. I leaned across and folded her chair before hoisting it over and laying it down in the sand for minimal safekeeping. While still sitting, we both took off our shirts and shoes, and then I looked at her with a question I didn't want to ask. How did she want to get down to the water? Hop across the sand in front of two dozen sunbathers, or have me carry her?

Again she read my mind. And without hesitation, she stood up on one leg, and then leaned over to lock her arms around my neck, shifting her weight onto my back.

"Giddy-up, hoss," she said, and I could feel the infectious smile behind my neck. I grinned and stood, adjusted her weight on my back, and then we half jogged across thirty yards of sand and into the white foam of low breakers.

We swam with the noncompetitive purpose of pleasure alone, for a while breaststroking, our faces popping up from the surface in slow rhythm, eyes blinking away salt water with each breath, and then letting the coolness wash over our faces again as we dipped our heads below. Then, at a distance from shore, we rolled over on our backs and floated, with our views of the sky the same: a cloudless canvas of blue like a porcelain cup covering our limited horizons. I could feel the movement of the sea, the rise and fall of deep waves.

As I sneaked a look over at Sherry, I saw that her eyes were open, but relaxed. I knew she was coming down from her earlier shot of adrenaline in the showdown with McKenzie. It was a rare pleasure to see her this way; I closed my eyes and enjoyed it.

Let her tell me what she wants to tell me, I thought. It might have been thirty minutes, it might have been an hour, but broken snatches of her voice finally brought me out of a trance.

"You know . . . kind of like . . . tell but didn't."

"What?" I said, rolling over and bringing my head and ears out of the water.

Sherry made the same maneuver and looked at me.

"Sorry. I was just talking out loud, I guess."

"Couldn't hear you, babe."

"The meet with Booker," she said. "Very odd."

We were now treading water next to each other about fifty yards from shore. We both turned toward land and did a kind of head-out-of-water stroke, slowly heading in.

"First, he tried to apologize for McKenzie and the other assholes, saying they didn't mean anything by it, and they weren't really such bad guys."

If it were possible to shake one's head in a bobbing sea, I shook my head.

"Then he said something about them being the kind of animals that see a weakness in their prey and go after it."

"What the hell was that about?" I said.

"Well, he tried to cover then by saying it was good police tactics, knowing the street, knowing the opponent."

"So the rest of those guys were cops?"

"I only recognized three or four of them. Mostly District Three, the area they call the danger zone," she said.

"And that's where Booker worked?"

"Yeah, it's been like some competitive club atmosphere out there for years—lots of macho shit. The captain in charge tries to keep a lid on it, but he also likes the image of being rough and ready. So he lets a lot go."

I kept stroking. Everybody knows that kind of culture exists in policing. It's natural, and sometimes even essential. You wouldn't want a bunch of schoolteachers trying to control a riot. You can't have a crew of desk jockeys running into a burning high-rise to carrying people down the smoking staircase. There's going to be a macho element in every department. You cook up a blend of testosterone, a heightened sense of authority, an emphasis on physical conditioning, and pepper it up with a dash of gun oil, and you can't avoid it. Good police management keeps it in check. I'd seen it in Philadelphia. I'd seen it fail in Philadelphia.

After a few minutes of silent swimming, I could see the sand below us. I stopped and stood. Sherry did the same on one leg, and then continued talking.

"The scuttlebutt has always been that a pack of these lifter cops are into steroids and uppers, but internal affairs can't—or won't—get involved. I sure wasn't going to get into that with Booker. So I changed the subject and asked him if he'd tried to do his physical therapy at the hospital rehab center. I told him it would be a lot more effective, that the specialists there know a lot more about range of motion and balance, instead of just muscle building."

"And?"

"It pissed him off. He said, 'Yeah, I could see how your range of motion helped you out back in the gym.' "

"So what are you going to report to your boss?" I asked.

"I don't know. The guy's got some rage, which is understandable. But he isn't doing the 'poor me' gig, or the self-loathing. He is however, pulling himself under for some reason. There's some kind of struggle going on inside, but who the hell knows what?"

As Sherry spoke, I watched her eyes. She was being more psychologically analytical with this guy Booker than I'd ever heard her be about her own situation. I caught myself thinking this might be a good thing for both her and him.

"Was he willing to talk with you again?"

"I didn't ask."

"Maybe you should."

"Yeah, maybe," she answered, and then turned back to the east, watching the roll of the sea, bouncing lightly on her foot and waving her palms underwater to stay balanced.

I moved in behind her and pushed my chest against her back and wrapped my arms around her.

"This is nice, eh?"

"Yeah," she said, relaxing against me, moving with the motion of the sea. "And I'm sorry about last night, Max."

"Yeah," I said. "I know."

8

ON FRIDAY, I ended up at Billy's, doing the kind of investigative research he always likes to foist on me.

"They say the criminal element will always be one step ahead of law enforcement, Max. But that's only because law enforcement spends so much time reacting instead of being proactive.

"By the time the DEA figured out that smugglers were sending cocaine inside hollowed-out railroad ties, they'd already moved on to molding the coke to look like plaster columns and sending it in as construction material.

"By the time the feds were warning people about identity fraud and keeping their social security numbers safe in their pockets, the hackers were already infiltrating the big data storage companies and pulling out millions of numbers for their own use."

I nodded, and let Billy go on in the kitchen while I sat out on the patio reading a sheaf of U.S. attorney and media reports he'd given me.

". . . the crime began when an employee at the Cleveland Clinic stole fifteen hundred Medicare patients' numbers and sold them to companies that billed the government about eight million in bogus health care claims . . ."

And another.

"'. . . while we know these numbers are being used by criminals . . . the criminals can use them again and again,'" said the U.S. attorney. "'That is a fundamental problem . . .'"

A newspaper clipping:

" . . . six Miami-Dade medical equipment suppliers are charged with sub-mitting eight million in bogus Medicare bills to insurance companies for services and equipment that were never provided to the patients. In turn, the Medicare system paid them about two and a half million . . ."

And yet another:

". . . in sworn testimony before the Senate Committee on Finance, a witness explained how she was able to set up a sham company with three thousand dollars and obtain a Medicare billing number, even though she had no prior experience, expertise, or discernable resources for providing durable medical equipment items or services. In the year her company operated, she was able to bill Medicare more than a million dollars . . ."

I had already closed the file by the time Billy came out onto the patio with a tall glass of vegetable juice in his hand and a smug look on his face, the kind you got from instructors or your parents when they were proud of teaching you something you didn't know.

"So, M-Max—what do you th-think? Motive?"

"A million bucks for shifting around a bunch of numbers?" I said. "Sure—goes on every day at the casinos, down at the track, and on Wall Street."

Billy looked askance, lifting his eyebrow. I knew he was a big-time investor, played the stock market on a daily basis. It was one of the things we differed on: He would argue that those who got in the financial game knew the rules and the nature of the beast, and thus took personal responsibility for their losses and gains. I would counter that the financial guys also knew the ways around those rules, not unlike the criminals who can crack safes and avoid surveillance cameras to get what they wanted. It was a subject we stayed away from.

"I m-meant do you think it would be m-motive enough to put Luz Carmen in physical danger, if she were tr-trying to expose such a scam and they f-found out?"

Now it was my turn to raise the eyebrow.

"Greed, Billy?"

We didn't need another symposium on how greed, sex, and power form the motivations for almost all the nasty thing humans do to one another.

"OK," he said. "Then I w-would suggest you go ahead with the surveillance of Ms. Carmen's br-brother, while I tr-try to track down some p-people I know with the FBI's white-collar crime pr-program in Miami."

"All right, boys," a woman's lilting voice came from inside. "I heard the phrase *FBI*, which means you're talking shop. I have not yet left for work—beware."

"Good morning, Judge," I said as Billy's wife, Diane, rattled around in the kitchen. "I didn't know you were still here."

She came out onto the porch dressed in a suit cut in the most conservative style, but the quality of the fabric and the way it was tailor-made to her petite frame was obvious even to a fashion slug like me. In her left hand, she held a china cup of steaming coffee.

"That fact does slip by a few of Billy's visitors," she said, hooking her right hand around Billy's upper arm and leaning her face into his shoulder. Billy looked down into her eyes with a grin only a loving husband can make seem natural.

"And you're complaining, madam?"

"Not a bit, baby," she said, and then with a knowing smile of her own, "but the less I know about what you two are up to, the better."

Both of our faces immediately broadcast innocence.

"Yeah, I thought so," she said. Then she gave Billy a kiss good-bye, and me a lesser one on the cheek.

"Lovely to see you, Max."

When the clicking sound of her heels on the tile to the front door diminished, I turned to Billy. "You're a lucky man, my friend."

"I am indeed."

Their marriage had not been an easy union. As a black kid from the projects who made it to the penthouse, Billy had a tendency in his law practice to snatch up cases of injustice. Diane McIntyre was a white woman of social standing who broke all her ensconced family's conservative social rules by becoming the first female judge in Palm Beach, where money, business, and brokered deals in smoke-filled back rooms have been a sitting foundation for more than a hundred years.

As an unemotional counselor, Billy had always answered my simple questions about how he and his wife are able to make it work with a smile and a statement: "Love, my friend M-Max, the kind no man can put asunder." A few hours later, I had a need to put something asunder, and love wasn't going to help me as much as a fifteen-shot 9 mm would have.

By 5:00 P.M., I was back in the parking lot of the West Boca Medical Complex, waiting to see if Andrés Carmen would come out. This time I was off to the side in the minor shade of a recently planted dogwood. I still don't know why they plant those skinny-trunk trees in the grass separators of parking lots. Aesthetics? Had to be; I've yet to see a Florida parking lot with big canopied trees providing acres of shade for customers.

At about 5:05 P.M., the end-of-the-day troop of employees began. Out the front doors came a bustling group that included several women dressed in those plain-cut pink scrubs that had made the transition from hospital surgery theaters and patient floors to the medical spin-off industries and learning campuses. Some of the men were similarly outfitted in blue. But I was looking for a slightly built young man with dark hair and a bit of a chin beard who'd be wearing a green version of this medical getup, the description Luz Carmen had given me of her brother.

At 5:10 P.M., I recognized Luz. She exited the building with that same careful look she had two days ago, her head on a swivel, scanning the parking lot, searching for someone who might be searching for her.

But this time, she was obviously with another woman, about her size, both of them dressed similarly in knee-length summer dresses and conservative short heels. They walked to a dark red Toyota Camry, and Luz got into the passenger side. I was relieved to see that she'd taken my advice and was getting a ride home with a co-worker. Maybe she was even staying with the other woman over the weekend, a suggestion Billy had made to her after I'd described the encounter in the park. If she noticed my pickup truck under the meager shade tree, she didn't show it. The friend pulled out, and they exited from the opposite side of the lot.

At 5:15 P.M., I spotted Andrés Carmen, walking with purpose out of the building, carrying a cardboard box a few books might fit into. He marched directly to a dusty white Toyota Corolla four rows back from the front and didn't look around to check the perimeter, as his sister had, nor did he make any "have a good weekend" small talk with co-workers, nor offer waves of good-bye to anyone. His face was stoic and calm as he unlocked the driver-side door and set the box over into the passenger seat before climbing in.

I started up my truck and then slipped into the exit lane behind him. My pickup is not the perfect vehicle for a tail. The color can draw attention and since the cab sits up, it's easier to spot in a rearview mirror. But I didn't detect any sense of watchfulness or concern on Andrés's part. If his sister had told him of the drive-by shooting on Wednesday, he wasn't showing any wariness. I kept a few cars back and as we wended our way out onto State Road 7 and headed south, I noticed that the only thing unusual about the young man's driving was that he stayed meticulously on the speed limit. And for a South Floridian, he had an unusual habit of using his turn signals, a nearly unknown form of etiquette in this part of the country.

After a half hour of trailing him, the only other hint that the kid might be acting unduly careful was his use of the secondary highway even though he was now well south into Broward County. I-95 would have been a lot quicker, even though it often clogs up at rush hour. Still, on this particular north-south corridor, you had to stop at every major intersection for traffic lights and folks turning into the endless shopping plazas, car dealerships, and fast-food restaurants.

If you were getting paid for your time on the road—which I was, as Billy's investigator—it was no big deal. But if you had someplace to go, it engendered the kind of drudgery or frustration that inevitably leads to road rage incidents, screaming matches through lowered windows, and the horn blowing that every city from New York to San Diego puts up with on any given day.

As a result, I was pleased to see that Andrés wasn't pulling any of that constant lane-changing or light-to-light turbo jumping that might gain you a car length in the grand scheme of things. I'd only had to endure three "dudes" with their woofers blasting through opened windows trying to impress with their bass music thumping. By the time Andrés finally pulled into a light industrial park in the city of Plantation, I was getting bored.

It seemed obvious that the boy was turning in a box full of patient identifications and maybe order records to someone up the line in the scheme his sister had outlined. And I was here only to document for Billy so he could connect enough dots to get the feds to pay attention. Still, when Andrés hit his signal and made another left turn into a covey of low-built offices and warehouses, the traffic flow cut down considerably; I had to drop back to avoid being obvious.

I let the kid get a couple of blocks ahead. When he pulled up into a parking spot in front of one of the businesses, I did the same and watched from a distance. Andrés got out of his Toyota Corolla with the cardboard box under his arm and again, without a glance to either side, walked into the building through a double glass door. I did a quick surveillance with a small pair of binoculars. The signage on the doors read BIOMECHANICS INC., with no names, proprietorship, or hours of operation. I jotted down the spelling and the address to turn over to Billy.

The cars already parked in front of the place were a Mercedes SL with a Florida plate and a Cadillac Escalade bearing a plate holder from a Dade County dealership I recognized. Again I noted the numbers for

Billy to track on the computer. Although some of the buildings in the block had garage-style doors for equipment loading, there was no such entrance for BioMechanics, and no trucks in the vicinity bearing their name or logo. If they were dealing with equipment, medical or otherwise, it wasn't being handled on this side of the building.

Then I did a quick assessment. I was parked in front of a place called Baseball City, USA, a warehouse with a glass-fronted entrance that advertised hours and days for indoor hitting practice, pitching machines, and on-site coaching for all ages. While I sat there, three boys about twelve or thirteen came out wearing cleats and hats and balancing aluminum bats on their skinny shoulders. A parent unlocked the side doors of a family-style van and the boys scrambled in, laughing and probably trading jibes over which of them had been whacking the baseballs harder, and who'd been whiffing for the past hour. While I was smiling at the thought of my own boyhood trips to a batting cage in South Philadelphia, my eye caught a glimpse of shiny green metal, just for a second, passing between buildings another block away. The color was too distinctive to be coincidental—the drive-by Monte Carlo.

I began a reassessment of the street: narrow, flanked by buildings. There were only other parked cars to duck behind for cover if bullets started flying; could be innocent children in the line of fire. I was about to hit my ignition: Before I'd let a drive-by occur, I'd park in front of Andrés's car, confront him inside the BioMechanics office, and blow my own surveillance. If the kid was indeed selling stolen patient info to some graft joint inside and my actions spoiled Billy's case, so be it.

My fingers were on the key when the door that Andrés had walked through opened, and a man stepped out, took a few steps into the street, and flipped open a cell phone. My fingers loosened on the key while I studied him. There was something familiar about him, though not the clothes. This guy's conservative slacks, open, white Oxford shirt, sleeves rolled to the elbows and bright against his dark skin, added up to a black man's Obama look. It was his carriage that betrayed him: He had that neighborhood slouch in his shoulders and hips, and that way of looking up and down the street without raising his head, not like he was looking for something expected, but for anything unexpected. All this gave me pause.

Back in the day when I was a Philadelphia beat cop, we used to fill out FI cards—field investigation notes on index cards—for anybody we considered suspect or worth keeping track of. We'd watch some guy hanging on a particular drug corner, or catch someone driving with their headlights off in a suspect area, and stop him, not for a violation, just a chat. We'd note his name, physical description, and take a Polaroid photo. "That's it, sir. Have a good day and if you don't belong here, don't come back." I'd had a whole box of FI cards, but I also had a good recollection for faces. It was old cop habit, one I couldn't kick. As I watched the guy down the street talk into his cell phone, I went through the FI box of street attributes in my head.

I didn't know this guy from Philly; it wasn't that far back. He wasn't a client of Billy's, but someone peripheral to a case I worked for my lawyer friend and colleague. This was a man used to checking out the streets, who was comfortable with it—a man who guarded his work.

A dealer—yes, a drug dealer from northwest Fort Lauderdale, one who'd actually helped me track down an animalistic killer who was targeting elderly women. The face flooded out of the past, followed by the name: The Brown Man. But what the hell was the Brown Man doing dressed like a casual businessman, hanging out at the location of a possible Medicare fraud office?

From my left, a Honda Odyssey rolled up in front of Baseball City and started disgorging half a dozen little leaguers. I hit the key to my ignition and pulled out to put my truck between them and the Brown Man. As I searched every possible corner for a flash of green, I could feel all the muscles in my neck and shoulders tighten with anxiety.

When I turned back to the Brown Man, I saw Andrés come out of the BioMechanics door, now empty-handed. The two men appeared to exchange a few words, and then split, Andrés into his car, the drug dealer into the office. When the white Corolla pulled out, I relaxed a bit and went back to surveillance mode. I gave Andrés a few hundred feet, and then eased my truck out to follow. We'd gone three blocks when the metallic green Monte Carlo yanked into view, the rumble of its engine guttural and ominous. When the car jumped in behind Andrés's, I was thinking only one thing: pursuit.

It took the kid about thirty seconds to figure what was going on. Once the Corolla hit the turn onto State Road 7, it bolted south without the slightest hesitation at the stoplight. Oncoming traffic screeched to a halt as the Monte Carlo rumbled unimpeded through the intersection. Stupidly, I was too far back; by the time I got close to the turn, irate drivers were already starting to inch forward. I cut the corner through a gas station driveway at a speed that turned several heads and elicited a "fuck you" from a patron. The move put me back on tail of the Monte Carlo.

Andrés had now pulled a Jekyll and Hyde as a driver. As patient and unhurried as he'd been on the roadway to make his delivery, he was now a madman. I kept my eyes fastened on the chrome of the Monte Carlo. But ahead of him, I could see dozens of brake lights flashing, and the roofs of vehicles skewing off to the left and right. I didn't bother to look at my own speedometer, but I knew from experience that in this kind of traffic and on this kind of road, our cars might have been hitting forty-five m.p.h. or fifty at certain stretches. But even those speeds were twice as fast as anyone else, and crazy enough to scare the shit out of everyone caught in the mix.

I worked my way up within a two-car length of the Monte Carlo's bumper and rode it, following like it was a snowplow in bad weather, thus avoiding the swerving commuters and obstacles slewing in its wake. The Monte Carlo's rear window was too tinted to see how many people were inside, or whether they had noticed me following. The only thing I could make out on the back window was a cartoon of a devilish-looking boy pissing on an oval Ford symbol. Somehow the insult seemed personal; I was starting to get angry.

We swerved through traffic. I knew these high-speed gigs didn't last long, despite the ones you see on most dangerous police videos. It was going to end soon, and badly. Trying to anticipate, I took a chance, looking up ahead as we approached another traffic light. Andrés's white Corolla jerked east, with the Monte Carlo following, cutting off a wall of vehicles and stomping out of the turn, smoke roiling out of its wheel wells as he punched it. I was caught in the cloud, unable to see a damn thing. As I waited for the inevitable jolt of some other blind driver hitting me, my stomach clenched. The scream of tire rubber and the blare of horns created a noise cloud of its own. All I could do was hold the line until we straightened out.

Now the kid was getting wild, searching like a trapped mouse for someway out: he'd start left, get cut off, and spin right. It wasn't working. The Monte Carlo was on him. I was on it. And no doubt a dozen people behind us were calling 911—fine with me. I just hoped the kid was smart enough to keep moving. Once he stopped, that automatic rifle that had been trained on me and his sister was going to start blasting. And this time, I was sure it wouldn't be firing into the trees.

My hope ended when the white Corolla pitched right, jumped a curb, and squealed into a neighborhood complex. We'd suddenly ducked out of traffic, but Andrés had isolated himself in a corridor of attached, two-story condos. There was one way in and one way out—no yards between the buildings. Zero lot lines. Zero choices. I saw him hit the cul-de-sac in front of the Monte Carlo and whip into a circle. It was a face off he could not win, so I punched it.

Two of the passengers in the Monte Carlo were halfway out of their car, rifles in hand, when my truck smashed into their trunk. Given that my bumper is set much higher, it buried into the green metal and sent the two men rolling into the street like tossed-away dolls. I'd long ago disabled my air bags, so I saw their weapons go clattering across the macadam. Still the jolt stunned me for a second, and the sight of the violent rear-ender must have done the same to Andrés. When I shook off the initial shockwave, I stared over the top of the Monte Carlo into Andrés's eyes. He hesitated, looked at me, and then started cranking his steering wheel.

As the Corolla started past, I caught movement from the back passenger-side door of the Monte Carlo, and punched my accelerator again until the whole tangled mess of metal and rubber started scraping across the pavement. The Monte Carlo's door stayed shut. I threw the truck into reverse and punched it again, cranking the wheel one way and then the other, trying to free the front end of my truck from the ass end of the Monte Carlo like some giant blue-black cat dragging a metallic green lizard from a neighborhood garden. Finally, bumpers tore loose and I was free.

But so were the inhabitants of the drive-by sedan—and they were armed. I kept the truck in reverse until I closed on the main road, and then U-turned it. I might have heard sirens in the distance, but I didn't hear gunfire. I shut out the voice that said someone might be hurt, and pulled out into traffic. In the vernacular that would surely show up in the police report, I fled eastbound.

9

BY THE TIME I reached I-95, my heart had stopped thrumming and my fingers had finally come out of their vise grip on the steering wheel. In my head, I ran the list of charges that a responding officer would soon be tallying: leaving the scene of an accident with injuries; reckless endangerment, including multiple moving traffic violations. I knew most major intersections in South Florida had video cameras mounted above their traffic lights. We'd probably blown through three of them during the chase. They'd have all our tag numbers and descriptions and, soon after that, our DMV records. If the first responding officers arrived on the cul-de-sac scene before the Monte Carlo got away—if the damn car was even drivable—they might get lucky and bust the occupants in possession of deadly weapons, which would make it easier to explain my role. But it still wouldn't be a free pass.

When the cops start pulling info from their computers, the first thing they'd get is my attorney's address. Billy's is the one I'd used on my Florida driver's registration as my home. What the hell else was I supposed to use, the longitude and latitude of my shack on the river? They'd be knocking on Billy's door within twenty-four hours.

I pulled over into the driveway of a gas station just before reaching the interstate entrance and watched an employee and two people pumping their own gas stare at the front of my truck as I parked. When the attendant sauntered over, I raised a palm to him to indicate I'd be with him in a minute; then I got on my cell. Billy's a preemptive strike kind of guy. I would need him eventually. It would be better to get him into the loop early. He answered on the third ring.

In all his roles as lawyer, friend, and a hell of a smart human being, Billy listens. His end of the conversation was nonexistent until I finished giving all the details I could of the last few hours. In his silence, I could almost hear his analytical mind at work. There was a long pause before he spoke.

"Max, from your directions to the cul-de-sac, you were in county jurisdiction. Go straight to the sheriff's office off Broward Boulevard and wait for me in the parking lot. We'll go in together. You'll turn yourself in."

I took a few seconds to think of what he was asking, conjuring up the scene in my head, thinking about the ripples: I did not enjoy an endearing reputation with the sheriff's office, having stuck my nose in some of their investigations in the past. And more than a few high-ranking officers knew of my relationship with Sherry. We'd long ago agreed not to blur the line between personal and professional agendas, but tongues wag in any organization. Then, of course, there was the possibility that I'd have to spend the night in jail. I'd hate like hell to have to do that again. But Billy was right. The alternative was to wait for them to come for me—that always turns out badly.

"OK, Billy," I finally said. "But what about the kid—you know they're going to track him down, too."

"I'm going to call Luz Carmen right now. If she knows how to get in touch with her brother, maybe she can convince him to do the same thing we're going to do," Billy said.

Good luck with that, I thought. "An illegal immigrant tied to a federal Medicare scam who's suddenly the target of a bunch of drive-by shooters isn't going to turn himself in, Billy."

"I said I'd ask her to try, Max. I'll give him the same opportunity as we're taking. He can come in with me."

I almost told him not to hold his breath.

"I'll be in the parking lot of the sheriff's office in an hour," I said instead, and hung up.

MY TRUCK WAS making a hell of a noise. I had to pull over twice to yank a warped fender away from the left front wheel to keep it from rubbing on the tire and setting up a burring wail, like an empty barrel being rolled down a back alley. The steering wheel was pulling hard to the right, a sure sign that a tie-rod was bent. The temperature gauge was running hot. I'd probably left a puddle of coolant on the street where I'd rammed the ass end of the Monte Carlo. I was staying off the main roads as best I could. It was dark now. I figured that even if a there was a "be on the lookout" with my truck's description and tag out on the police radio, I might be safe for an hour. A few blocks from the sheriff's office I pulled into the Dunkin' Donuts shop and parked as deep in their lot as I could, to stay out of sight. If I was going to jail, I wasn't going on an empty stomach.

Not the most popular spot at 8:00 P.M., the doughnut shop was nearly empty when I walked in. There was an old guy in the back wearing a tattered-wool winter coat, even though it was eighty-four degrees outside. His gray hair was matted, and he was having a hushed conversation with someone who appeared to be at the bottom of his Styrofoam coffee cup. There was no one within earshot.

A couple of tables away, a younger version of the same sad story was lounging in a corner. His head was shaved on two sides, but he'd left a strip of oiled-up black hair running down the middle. He was wearing dirty jeans and a pair of black-and-white sneakers that looked like a rip-off of the old Chuck Taylors; I winced to see such tradition fall so low, even if they were fakes. The kid was balancing a cigarette on his lip and looked up when I came in, but his focus was on the counter girl, not me. Dramatically, he checked his watch and rolled his dull eyes at her. The "hurry the fuck up and let's get outta here" message was clear.

I stepped up and ordered a large coffee with cream and sugar and two blueberry cake doughnuts. The girl nodded her bleach blonde head at me but didn't move at first. Her dark eyes were looking up at the top of my forehead instead of in my face, and when I widened my own eyes in question, she reached over and pulled a wad of napkins from the dispenser next to us, handing them across the counter.

"You need a napkin for that?" She was still looking up past my eyes.

When I took the wad and wiped at my forehead, the napkins came back smeared with blood. I wiped some more, and then looked at the girl, who was watching with an expression that said she was a little embarrassed for me.

"Good?" I said.

Her fingers came up to a spot along her own temple, and I mocked the gesture, wiping away more blood. I must have split my skin open when my head hit the windshield after colliding with the Monte Carlo. I'd never even felt it.

The girl nodded when I'd apparently wiped away enough of my blood to be presentable, and then repeated my order. I gave her a five for the $2.30 bill and left the change as I took my order and walked to a table as far from the other two occupants of the store as possible. As I passed him, the boyfriend watched me from under eyebrows pierced with small silver rings. When I winked at him, he turned away sullenly. It was only after I'd sat down and pried the lid off my coffee and took a sip that I noticed that my hands were dirty from pulling at the wheel well of my truck, fingers and palms dusty with a rust-colored film. I got back up and headed into the men's room.

The older guy in the back was still staring into the bottom of his cup, and his fingers were stained with more grime than my own, their blunted tips caressing the Styrofoam. As I got closer, the shabbiness of his clothing became more apparent, and I could see he was wearing a worn baseball cap with AIG stitched on the front. He was muttering something about "sub-prime credit default swap derivatives."

I went into the restroom and locked the door behind me. When I looked in the mirror, I saw a haggard, dirty, and unexpectedly older-

looking face staring back. Granted, I am not used to looking into mirrors. My river shack out on the edge of the Glades doesn't have one. At
Sherry's, I shave by touch in the shower, feeling my way through the
process with the tips of my fingers instead of looking for missed spots.
I've always done it that way.

When I looked at my reflection now to see if I'd removed all the
blood, I was slightly surprised by the dark bags under my gray-colored
eyes. There were prominent crow's-feet at the corners that I didn't recall
being there before. My skin was tanned recently from long runs on
the beach and from the canoeing I did to and from my semi-isolation
on the river, before I spent much time at Sherry's. I cranked a sheet of
paper towel from the dispenser on the wall and moistened it beneath
the faucet.

After wiping away some flecks of blood still on my forehead, I in-
spected the split. It wasn't deep, but the dark color of a slight contusion
was growing just below it. Satisfied, I brushed back my brown hair, only
to see more of the gray at my temples. Again, I was stupidly surprised:
What, Max, you didn't think you were aging out there in the Glades?

Yes, I am a pirate, two hundred years too late

The lyrics came into my head even though I'm not even a big Jimmy Buffett fan. The line about being an over-forty victim was too
self-pitying. I finished up and went back out into the store, where I sat
back down at my table and drank my coffee. As I took a few decent
swallows of the now cooled-down brew, I reminded myself I still had
a case to work.

In my mind, I reviewed what I had so far: A paranoid woman pres-
ents herself as a whistle-blower on a scheme to rip off Medicare funds,
but she's afraid to go to the feds—why? Because she's illegal, or because
her brother's involved, and he's illegal? If true, where's the motivation to
rat out the scam to begin with? If they're both illegal and flaunting the

law by working without documentation, what does it matter to her if someone on the side is ripping off her adopted government?

I have an automatically cynical attitude about people who simply do the right thing because it's the right thing. Human beings work on age-old motivations: greed, self-preservation, protection of family or those close to them. Seldom, I believe, do they give themselves up for the greater good.

Billy says I'm a sad person for carrying such thoughts. I say it makes me careful.

Say we have a good soul who's trying to do the right thing, but also to protect her brother. When we follow him, we spot the Brown Man, a known drug dealer. What the hell is he doing with his fingers in a Medicare scam? The players are suddenly getting shadier.

Then after our new addition, the Brown Man, just happens to make a cell call, along comes the Monte Carlo AK-47 shooters, who were obviously put onto some kind of contract to do away with our friend Andrés Carmen. Though these players are about as rough as they come, dumb-ass Max gets involved anyway, ruins his truck, and is now sought by the cops. Meanwhile, the kid he tried to save is probably on his way back to South America by now.

In half an hour, I'm going to have to spill all this to save my own ass from a night in the county jail. Maybe it'll fly, and maybe it won't. Just on the edge of saying "I don't need this shit," I decided that just in case I was looking at lockup, I'd better eat something. But when I picked up the wax-covered bag of blueberry cake doughnuts, I could tell just by the weight that something wasn't right. I opened the top and peered inside; there was now only one doughnut inside.

I'm not so old yet that I worry about losing my mind. I'm positive that the counter girl did indeed put two in there. When I looked around, I saw the old AIG guy still sitting there, discussing high finance with his cup, though there were new flecks of crumblike detritus in his matted beard. I just shook my head, drained my coffee, then picked up the bag with the remaining doughnut inside, and dropped it on AIG's table as I left. Behind me, I heard the old man mutter something that sounded like "provide additional liquidity" along with the crinkling of the bag being reopened.

WHEN I GOT to the eight-story sheriff's administration building, I again looked for a spot in the rear of the lot and then parked nose in. The actual garage area was down the block, so only a few squad cars were nearby. There were mostly civilian employees and detectives on this side, and they wouldn't be aware of the BOLO alerts being put out on the radio describing my truck. I rolled down my windows. I had the automatic power windows disabled and cranks installed when I bought the truck. Even though the engineers tell you the electricity will keep running to your windows when you dive into one of the millions of canals in South Florida that run alongside the roads, I don't trust them. If I go into the water, I'm gonna be able to roll down the window myself and climb out.

A night air blew in, filled with the odors of auto exhaust and daily dust, of standing water and heated asphalt. I swore I picked up the faint scent of cigar smoke, which caused me to look around for a glowing tip along the car roofs, but I saw nothing. How long does a distinct puff of air last before it gets dispersed and assimilated into the common atmosphere? I once read a science magazine article that claimed we have all been breathing the same recycled air molecules since the beginning of time. Every one of us has the chance of sucking a molecule that once came out of Shakespeare's mouth. Oh, rapture. At 9:42 P.M., my cell phone rang, with Billy's number on the screen.

"Yeah?"

"You're in the parking lot," he said.

"Southeast corner."

"I'll drive around."

A minute later when I saw his Mercedes make the corner, I flashed my lights once. He started my way, and I got out and stood in the lot while he backed into a spot. He joined me, dressed in a conservative dark suit complete with a carefully knotted tie.

"M-Max. You are not l-looking well," Billy said, readjusting his usual greeting while taking my measure from head to foot.

"Yeah, funny how that happens," I said as I shook his extended hand.

Following his lead, we started walking toward the front entrance.

"I sp-spoke to Assistant Chief Hammonds, who has graciously agreed to m-meet with us."

"Pretty high up the food chain for a leaving the scene and a handful of moving violations," I said. Billy stared straight ahead and kept walking.

"I w-would not be m-much of a lawyer if I didn't have c-connections, Max."

"Yeah. And how much info did you promise to feed him if he agreed to handle this?"

"I believe the ch-chief has followed your c-career, M-Max: the abducted children, the serial killer, the b-bodies in the Glades. He is a m-man who knows the value of information. In a s-situation like this, you do not deal with clerks."

I looked at the side of Billy's face, and I believe he felt my look on his skin.

"I know how elitist that s-sounds, Max. B-But I am trying to keep you out of jail."

"How much do we tell him?"

"You tell him nothing," Billy said. "I w-will do the talking."

After we emptied our pockets of all metal objects, cell phones, and foil-wrapped chewing gum, we walked through a metal detector and were directed to a Plexiglas enclosure we used to call a fishbowl. After Billy told the officer inside of our appointment with Chief Hammonds, she made a call to confirm, and then took our driver's licenses through a slotted drawer akin to a bank teller's. Then she directed us, one at a time, to stand before a camera to have our photos taken.

I shook my head. I knew from previous experience that there were no prisoners housed in this building, and if there were any criminals inside, they were most likely being interviewed with a half a dozen detectives surrounding them—but hell, yes, safety first.

While the aide printed out photo ID visitor's badges, I looked up from the marble inlaid floor to the eight-story atrium, the ceiling soaring up into a grand dome. Like Fort Knox with a gilded courthouse decor, I thought. The security consultants had watched too many reruns of *Assault on Precinct 13* and the planners studied too much Roman Architecture 101.

Finally, we were given a fifth-floor room number and directed through a now unlocked pair of heavy glass doors to the elevator.

"You've been here before, right?" I said to Billy.

"N-Not on a traffic violation."

"Not to the fifth floor."

"N-Not on a traffic violation," Billy repeated.

When the elevator doors opened, we were met by a thin man in civilian dress: oxford shirt, tie, suit pants, and polished loafers.

"Gentlemen," he said. "I'm Detective Sergeant Meyers."

No hand was offered, by either Meyers or us.

"Chief Hammonds will see you in his office," Meyers said as we followed him through a slight maze of beige-colored hallways and through two doors, before our guide stopped in front of an office and rapped lightly on the door.

"Come," was the answer from the other side. The voice and phrase made me think of Sean Connery in a submarine movie. Meyers opened the door and let us pass first. The room was small, with a big desk that took up most of the space. The dominating presence of the man standing behind it seemed to take up the rest.

"Chief," Billy said, reaching across the desk and shaking the man's hand, which enveloped Billy's like a catcher's mitt, "this is M-Max Freeman, sir. I believe you've met."

Hammonds had been a couple of ranks lower when we'd crossed paths in the past. He'd been the lead on Sherry's case involving the abducted children. During that investigation, Hammonds had used me as bait to finally draw out the killer. I didn't hold the tactic against him. He'd done what he thought he needed to do to stop a serial killer.

I extended my hand without reservation. The chief was as tall as me, but a good fifty pounds heavier. And even though I couldn't see his legs below the desktop, my guess was that the majority of his weight was in his barrel chest and draft horse butt.

"Mr. Freeman," he said, taking my hand. I doubted that the chief shook the hands of most criminals turning themselves in. "It's been a while."

I simply nodded. Usually, I like occupying the upper ground, but in this instance I was in the position of depending on others to decide my fate. With a wave of his huge paw, the chief directed us to two chairs flanking his desk. The detective sergeant remained standing behind us. When I glanced over my shoulder, it looked suspiciously as if he were guarding the door to block any escape—which made me nervous. Hammonds knew of my background as a Philadelphia cop, and hence realized that putting a desk between us and a man behind me would set any cop's teeth on edge.

Once we were seated, he wasted no time.

"Gentlemen, after Mr. Manchester's call, I did some checking. Traffic enforcement does indeed have several digital photographs of what is being described as a three-vehicle chase being executed through heavy evening traffic, and causing multiple rear-end collisions as other innocent drivers were forced to take defensive measures to avoid those vehicles," Hammonds said, glancing down at a sheaf of paper in front of him, but mostly holding my eyes.

"We then have reports from our patrol officers on what appears to have been the terminus of that chase in the fourteen hundred block of Southwest Forty-fifth Court, where one of said vehicles was disabled, and upon arrival of several squad cars, abandoned. Foot pursuit of at least four individuals resulted in the arrest of three. The fourth is still in the wind, but I'm confident we'll find him."

No doubt of that, I thought. Hammonds was an old bull, a cop who looked the part of a warrior who started in the street and then worked his way up the line, learning political tricks along the way to reach up into the ranks where a less ambitious officer would never tread, nor care to. He made no attempt to cover his gray hair, nearly white, in fact, at the temples. His jowls hung loose, and he had a way of keeping his massive hands clasped in front of him on the desk. He didn't flex or point, and didn't use his hands to talk for him or with him. They lay instead in a pile before him, their size and potential enough to catch and keep your eye. I thought of sleeping dogs and the time-honored warning not to rouse them.

"Also included in the report, gentlemen, is the confiscation of, uh, let me see . . ." he hesitated for maximum effect, "three submachine guns, one being an AK, which we don't often see out on the streets; two large caliber handguns concealed in draw holsters mounted under the seats; and in a false compartment behind the glove box, a substantial amount of cocaine.

"Those now in custody account for a long rap sheet for drug-related arrests, including sales and distribution, and the requisite add-ons such as aggravated assault, robbery, and resisting arrest. One of them is particularly well known as a past enforcer for a drug crew, which, to our knowledge, has not been active for more than five years. The crimes these three have committed are from the past, gentlemen. They've been lying low, or have been engaging in activities that we haven't caught up with yet. But the weapons found at the scene are disturbing, as is a box officers found in the trunk of their disabled car, which contained a substantial amount of prescription drugs, including amphetamines and steroids."

I looked over at Billy who seemed to be assessing the information laid out before us as unemotionally as if the chief were reading from the telephone directory.

"Help us, gentlemen, and as the game goes, we shall endeavor to help you," Hammonds said in a voice that clearly indicated his play was on the table.

After a full thirty seconds, as Billy put his mental filing cards in order, he opened his hand. "First of all, this entire incident took place while Mr. Freeman was in my employ, w-working as my investigator. During a pl-planned surveillance, Mr. Freeman deemed that it would be prudent to f-follow a certain individual to gain intelligence on his p-possible connections to a client's case."

"And your client's case is drug-related?" Hammonds said.

"It w-wasn't until today," Billy said. "My client is a wh-whistle-blower on a Medicare fraud scheme. The man in the lead car is someone we surmised was transporting records pertaining to that enterprise. During his surveillance, Mr. Freeman determined that this person of interest was indeed in danger. Thus Mr. Freeman took steps to aid him."

"And was there probable cause for Mr. Freeman to assume such danger?" Hammonds said.

"A pr-previous drive-by shooting," Billy answered, "in Mr. Freeman's pr-presence, in Palm Beach County. My client was the target."

Hammonds gave himself the same thirty seconds of silent thoughtfulness that Billy had given himself. The guy behind us never moved. I watched the chief's eyes. I could tell he was thinking advantage, figuring politics, working it like a poker hand.

"Well, that's quite a story. I'll grant you that," Hammonds finally said. "But it doesn't do shit for me."

I've always admired the way some people can switch their syntax and vocabulary, not to mention their manners, at the drop of a dramatic hat. I wonder if they practice in front of a mirror like DeNiro in *Taxi Driver:* "You talkin' to me?"

Whether or not the chief's tone caught Billy off-guard was impossible to tell. His face remained professionally stoical as Hammonds continued.

"The Medicare scam is joint state and federal, Counselor. The FBI might be interested, but I'm not. The drive-by was in someone else's jurisdiction. No good to me. I don't need to know your client's name since I already have, uh, Andrés Carmen's," Hammonds said, looking down at his sheaf of paper again. "I doubt that Mr. Carmen is your client, Mr.

Manchester, you don't do that kind of work. And I know Mr. Freeman doesn't hang his ass out for some small-time drug sniffer." Hammonds had shifted his gaze to me. I shrugged.

"My guess is that this Carmen is a relative of your client, Counselor. Mother? Young wife with child?" he said to Billy. "You're a bleeding heart, Counselor. But even up in the judicial hierarchy, people know your leanings only go so far."

The not-too-guarded reference to Billy's wife might have set another man's teeth to grinding. Instead, he laid out what we had to offer.

"What we can give you, Chief, is the location of the w-warehouse building, in your jurisdiction, where Mr. Freeman witnessed the exchange of information. We can give you the name of a prominent drug distributor from one of your districts who obviously has ties to the fraud scheme and quite possibly the movement of prescription drugs you've now confiscated."

The chief again took his full thirty seconds to consider. It was a game everyone played: pimps, prosecutors, confidential informants, detectives, judges, and witnesses.

"Very well, gentlemen," Hammonds finally said, standing up. "If you give that information to Detective Meyers on the way out, Mr. Freeman will still be receiving a summons for leaving the scene of an accident, but his able attorney can just mail in the fine."

After Billy nodded, we all stood. The game was over; the winner would be determined at a later date. As we headed for the door, Hammonds came around his desk and said, as he placed a condescending hand on my shoulder, "Max! How is Sherry doing these days? I mean, with her recovery and all?"

I turned, maybe a bit too fast, the movement causing the hand to slip from the fabric of my shirt. Even when looking directly into the man's eyes, I couldn't read them. Hammonds's face gave no indication whether the question about Sherry was truly an innocent inquiry of a fellow cop; or a warning that the deputy chief knew all about me, a subtle declaration he had some measure of control over me.

"She's doing fine, Chief," I said. "I'll let her know you were asking about her."

After we walked out into the hallway, the chief's door was closed softly behind us, the sound of its quiet snicking making me feel it wouldn't be long before I was back here again.

When I left Billy in the parking lot, he said he'd continue trying to call Carmen to warn her that there was a BOLO out on her brother's car, and that he would be arrested if he was stopped. If the kid was illegal, he'd be looking at deportation. And that was the good news. If the guys who were after him found him first, he'd be dead.

On the way to Sherry's I stopped at the 7-Eleven, again parking in the shadows, even though Hammonds said I was off the hook for now. I went in looking for a six-pack of Rolling Rock and was disappointed that they were out of bottles. I had to settle for the cans. I hate drinking beer out of metal; it's so damned uncouth.

Back in my truck, I popped the first one, trying to relax and let some of the anxiety go down with the taste of alcohol on the back of my throat. Hammonds was old and cagey. I didn't see him as the kind to give someone like me a free pass for nothing. He's more the kind who works the system 24/7. In each new situation, he'd take away an advantage. Every person who entered his universe had a possible use. I knew guys like him back in my life as a Philly cop. They were ambitious. They were political. They didn't give without getting back. It was the way of their world. Oh, we were going to dance again, Hammonds and I. I was going to have to tighten my moves.

I was halfway down the street toward Sherry's when my fan belt started making a hell of a squealing noise. Even I was wincing at the shrill sound as I eased the truck up her driveway. I went inside from around back as usual, but the pool was silent. The patio doors were unlocked, and the only light on was the stove overhead. I locked up behind myself and found Sherry in the bedroom, lying on top of the covers with her mirror, staring at two legs.

"Hi," I said, pulling the tab on one of the beers. The sharp crack of aluminum sounded like something breaking. Sherry hadn't looked up at my greeting but turned her head to the sound.

"Since when do you go for cans," she said, her tone carefully non-accusatory. I looked at the container as if I'd just discovered it in my hand.

"Yeah, you're right. I always said I'd rather have a bottle in front of me . . ."

"Than a frontal lobotomy," Sherry finished the old saw, but she was smiling when she did so.

I kicked off my Docksides, sat down on the edge of the bed, and propped my back against the headboard.

"Or maybe you just like the sound of crunching metal these days?" she said as she looked back down at her mirror, avoiding eye contact. I looked at the side of her face and noted the pinching of skin at the corner of her eye; she was having fun at my expense. I stayed silent and waited her out, a small victory.

"Well, I am a cop," she finally said.

"So how'd you hear?"

She looked over and let the smile escape. "I have my sources."

"Right! Any single woman cop who's a pretty, long-legged blonde is going to have sources on the job who are interested in besmirching the character of the present boyfriend," I said, matching her smile.

But something I said caused a flickering deep behind her eyes. She pushed it back, and then shook her head "All right, Mr. PI, a couple of uniforms did recognize the description of your truck on the radio and called me to see if you'd gone off your meds," she said, slipping back into teasing mode. "The old beast didn't sound too good when you pulled up."

I took another hit of the Rolling Rock. "I won't be filing an accident claim," I said. "But my guy up at the body shop on Indiantown Road is going to get some business."

Silent again, I watched the aqua glow from the pool flow through the bedroom window and dance on the ceiling.

"You gonna tell me what happened?" Sherry said.

I took another drink and laid it out for her, from the time I started tailing Andrés Carmen, until I left Chief Hammonds's office. Like most good detectives, Sherry's a good listener. She let the story come out without interruption, and in the end said, "Jesus, Max."

"Yeah, I think I said the same thing a couple of times tonight."

Sherry reached over and put her hand on the side of my face, slid her fingers into my hair, and gave me one of those "poor baby" looks. The show of affection was nice. Though I've never been one who expects the whole sympathy thing, everybody's human.

I took her hand and kissed her palm. "I love you, baby," I said.

"I know you do, Max. Sometimes I just don't know how you can."

10

OK, ENOUGH OF *what if*, Booker. You've got to stop talking to yourself: What's done is done. You've got to catch up and live in the real world. Right?

Yeah, but in the real world, people are walking around on two fucking legs. You're not. In the real world, people can walk up a set of stairs. In the real world, you used to squat three hundred pounds, and now you can't even climb out of this chair on your own.

All you can remember are those goddamned dimmed headlights, knowing they were going way too fast, and that total lack of screeching brakes. And hey, guess what, your stupid life did not flash in front of your eyes. You just reacted. They say you jumped, and that's what saved your life, such as it fucking is. Next thing you know, you're lying in a hospital bed and you wake the hell up and get as much of a grip on what's happened as you can, given that when you look down there's no lumps in the sheets below your waist.

Fuck it, you don't even want to look—so you don't. For days, you don't. Even after the docs come in and give you all that bullshit about how amputees can do anything anyone else can. And they know it's a shock, but medical science has come such a long way . . . blah, blah, blah.

So you're pissed. And you're always gonna ask: Why you? Who the hell did this to you? And you hold on to that anger 'cause you know what? It makes you feel a little bit alive. Why the hell haven't they caught the rat bastard who did this to you? Six months and they can't find a car thief? Hey, I'm a cop, too. And every cop, not just the fucking detectives, knows that people repeat a story like mine. It gets told in some sleazy shooting gallery somewhere, some fucking bar, on some

shit-heel corner with a bunch of losers hanging out smoking and trying to build themselves up, so they can be better than the loser next to
them: "Hey, man, you seen that shit on TV about the cop who got his
legs chopped off on I-595? Whoa, awesome, dude."

"Yeah, I heard Jimmy the Fuckup did it."

"No way, Jimmy the Loser? That kid who's always stealin' cars when
he's fuckin' high?"

"Yeah, Petey the Prick said he was doin' forties with Jimmy and he
told him he was all fucked up and drivin' an old boosted Chevy and
smacked ass into the back of somebody on the freeway and pinched that
cop and just got out and boogied."

"No shit. Did Petey turn him in, man? There's a big fucking reward
out for anyone rats the dude out. If Petey didn't, I sure as hell will."

Which is why you gotta be even more pissed—I mean, come on!
The sheriff's office put a fifty-thousand-dollar reward for information
out there a week after it happened, and they haven't gotten a single
lead worth a damn? Fuckups talk when something like that goes down.
Somebody's gotta hear something—unless it wasn't just some fuckup.

I mean, you have to wonder about the forensics on the thing. When
the so-called detectives who are working the case come to you and say
they couldn't lift a single usable print off the inside of the car that almost killed you? A screwup like some Jimmy the Loser doesn't go to
the trouble of wearing surgical gloves and wiping down the interior of
the car he's joyriding in for the night. They couldn't find any hair? No
fibers? No empty Buds in the back seat with DNA all over the mouth of
the bottles? Come on, man!

All right, all right, Marty, calm yourself; you're a real cop. You know
that CSI television is bullshit. But you gotta wonder, don't you? Yeah,
you listened to the shrinks talk on and on about the anger and frustration that's normal after an amputation, the anxiety and all that shit—
and how this is all an ongoing gradual process. But what about those
guys at the gym? What happened there? What? They don't want to
associate with a gimp wheelie? You were tight with those guys, and now

they are definitely pulling away. Yeah, you know things were getting a little hinky about the other thing. But shit, they were your boys, liftin' and studdin' over at Marbury's together, man. Maybe you were getting a little away from the drugs and stuff, but you weren't gonna spoil it for the rest of them. They understood that, didn't they—all except that asshole McKenzie, anyway.

Ha! McKenzie. Wasn't that a kick when that Richards broad came in and showed that fucker up on the dip bars? Little prick turning red in the face, blowing like some kinda wounded cow, while she just kept on kicking out the reps. Man, the woman was impressive. But what was up with that anyway, her coming down to shoot the shit? You knew the department shrinks would get around to it sooner or later, trying to find a way to dig inside your head and get you to "accept." You were all ready to blow her off, too, but there was something about her, and not just because she's a wheelie like you. When you were talking at the café, man, it wasn't like she was trying to psychoanalyze you. It was more like she was asking questions that she needed some answers, too, you know. I mean, you ain't stupid. You know they sent her in. But she ain't bad to look at, and with that display on McKenzie, you gotta respect the lady's workout ethic, right? And everybody's heard about that time she put a 9 mm in that serial killer dude's face. Righteous shoot. You gotta like a girl like that.

But you also gotta watch it. They tried to get a lot of internal affairs guys into the gym before, and we always smelled them out. What makes her different—because she's missing a leg? You gotta be careful, man. And you were, right? All you talked about at the café was that stuff about the forensics, and why the hell they hadn't found the guy who fucking rammed you. And she said she'd ask around. That can't hurt, her being a detective and all.

So you make a date, right? She gave you her cell. Meet her at the café again. Why not?

11

To say that Billy Manchester and I were rolling down an asphalt lane through a decrepit mobile home park at dawn in Billy's Lexus is enough to say that this case had become unique. The sun had not yet surfaced from the edge of the Atlantic Ocean when I met Billy, on his insistence, at his building. He'd called at the uncharacteristic hour of five in the morning:

"Max, I need you to get here as soon as possible. We have a seven A.M. appointment with Ms. Carmen and her brother."

Billy does not do this kind of thing—I do. It's what PIs do: Meet with the scumbags, hook up in the alleys, and sit with coffee for hours on surveillances. The attorneys don't do this, especially Billy. Just look at him: He's dressed down this morning in a light, camel-hair sport coat and tailored poplin trousers. His white shirt is impeccably pressed. He deigned to leave the tie at home.

"I was able to reach Ms. Carmen late last night, and told her that if she had any way to contact her brother, she should do it. At four this morning, she called and said she was meeting with him here, and begged me to come," Billy said, looking out beyond the headlights in the still neighborhood.

I knew he was concentrating. He rarely drives. Hell, he rarely leaves his apartment unless he's in court or walking to lunch along Clematis Boulevard in downtown West Palm Beach. His eyes were focused. When he's concentrating, he can lose the stutter in someone's presence. Even I take note, because it's as if you weren't even there. But I don't take it personally.

"Now I fear he's put his s-sister in harm's way," Billy said.

I looked at the side of his face but withheld my urge to respond: "Duh, you think so?"

"It is an enduring tragedy to see what family will do to one another," he said. Having an intimate knowledge of Billy's upbringing, I kept my mouth shut.

We'd slowed to a near crawl as Billy's GPS system announced, "Destination two hundred feet, at 320 Harriett Street." The pleasant computer voice was highly inappropriate for the milieu of sagging, broke-back trailers, autos up on cinder blocks, rotting fences failing in their attempt to offer some privacy from the trailer next door, and the ubiquitous scarred picnic table set out on a grassless strip of yard as a respite from what it must be like inside each home.

"There's her car," I said to Billy when I spotted Luz Carmen's little red Toyota in the driveway ahead. He pulled perpendicular to her car, with just enough room to open his driver's door. She would not be leaving before we did. Billy turned his car alarm on manually before getting out, thus foregoing the bleeping sound of doing it with his remote. When I joined him at the side of Carmen's car, there was just enough sunlight to see the address of the trailer spray-painted on a piece of plywood covering the front windows. It had been a year since the last hurricane. Most people took down even their minimal barricades against the storm to let the light in and reconnect with the view. But when I surveyed the trash-strewn landscape around us, I figured even that act of procrastination might have made sense in this case.

There were no obvious lights in three windows on our side of the trailer. I'd been in a few of these tin cans before and worked the layout in my head: kitchen at the south end where plywood covered the small front bow of paned glass, living area behind the entrance door, bedroom or bedrooms at the north end. Billy stepped up onto the cinder blocks that formed a stairway to the base of the door. Before he could raise his hand to knock, I heard a low roll of guttural vocal cord, vibrating just enough to be audible. Both of us looked to our left and saw the muddy yellow-brown eyes of a pit bull watching us from the inside of a low fence.

Even in the low light, I could see the whitened slashes of scar tissue across the mutt's face, but also the ripple of muscle in its neck and front quarters. The dog turned its head just so, with the kind of curious look you find endearing in some species. But in this one, it seemed more like that of a beast assessing which mouth-size chunk of human calf it'd like to chew into first. There would be no advanced warning of a bark or howl that would spoil its inherent surprise. This was the kind of dog that comes up in silence and buries its teeth deeply before you realize it. Billy looked at me and then rapped lightly on the metal door.

On the third try, Luz Carmen opened just wide enough to let in a sliver of sunrise that illuminated her face. Once she was sure we weren't a SWAT team or warrant servers, she stepped back. As we entered, the smell was the first thing that slapped me.

If there is an odor of unfettered and decadent despair, this was it: the ripeness of soiled fabric, the sweat of unwashed bodies, the fetid smell of spoiled food, and the sweet cut of marijuana smoke, all muddled by a cloying overlay of burning incense. The room was lit only by the glow of a big-screen television and shards of the sunrise leaking in through the kitchen windows. On a worn couch, a kid about fourteen worked an Xbox remote. He was thin and dark. Though I thought his head was wet, later I realized that the long black locks were simply greasy.

He did not look up, at first, as we shuffled into the limited space, his eyes intent on the television screen, his fingers moving precisely on the control buttons. Luz Carmen did not bother to introduce us, and instead stepped back into the kitchen area, drawing us with her. I cut my eyes to the hallway to the left, watching for movement, for the brother, for any sign of threat. The far-too-confining space inside the trailer put me on edge.

Luz Carmen folded her arms over her chest, gripping her elbows. "Mr. Manchester, please," she began, looking down, unwilling to meet Billy's eyes. "There are people after my brother. They want to kill him, and it is my fault. If I had not gone to you, this would not be happening. You have to help us." Though her voice was raspy and wet, her words sounded less like a request than a demand.

I turned my eyes to watch the side of Billy's face, deferring to his silence. Behind him, dirty dishes were stacked in the sink and the drain board. Open beer cans tumbled out of a yellow recycling bin on the floor near his polished loafers.

"No, I don't have to help you," Billy said in his own voice, the real thing compared to Carmen's. "I d-don't need to do anything, Ms. Carmen. I can walk out of here and l-let them kill you, your br-brother, and anyone else involved."

Luz Carmen looked up; her eyes widened as if she'd been slapped.

"I can c-call the authorities, give them this address, and have you arrested for conspiracy to commit grand theft. And all of you are harboring a fugitive," Billy said with the same conviction, hooking his thumb back toward the couch.

"Hey, what the hell, man," the kid on the couch said, and started to get up.

I turned and pointed a finger at him. "Sit down and shut up." He lowered himself back down and kept his hands on the remote. Under his breath, he said something that sounded like "fucking cop." I let it go, but from then on I kept cutting my eyes to him to make sure his fingers never left the controller. I was unarmed and wanted to know that no one else in the place was, either.

"Ms. Carmen," Billy continued. "You p-put yourself in danger. You p-put my investigator in danger. You did this by not telling m-me the depth of your brother's involvement in all of this, and the m-methods by which he and his friends are running this operation."

"They are not his friends," Luz Carmen said, but in a smaller voice. Hers was a need to argue, to defend, to hang on to even a shard of the pride that had seen her through difficult times. But she was starting to break, and I knew that Billy would have to be careful not to take her over that line.

"Call your br-brother out here, Ms. Carmen, so we can tr-try to work something out," Billy said.

Again she stared at the floor, but nodded her head, and then called out: "Andrés, *por favor.*"

He appeared out of the darkness of the hallway, a scarecrow of a boy barely taller than his sister. His hands were empty, and he approached with a limp. There was a bandage taped onto his forehead, and his left eye was circled by purpled and swollen skin. He still tried to carry some strut, with his lips pinched tight, and his eyes holding a ridiculous glare, considering his battered face.

I immediately assessed him as not presenting a threat. Up close, he looked impossibly young: The skin on his face that wasn't bruised was smooth and clear, and his soft dark eyes matched his sister's. He was actually dressed in one of those blue hospital scrub tops like the ones at the medical building, and his skinny arms hung from the short-sleeved armholes like sticks from a melting snowman. With his empty hands and injured gait, I figured I could drop him with a single punch. I tried to relax my face and posture, to become nonthreatening myself.

"Andrés, this is my lawyer, Mr. Manchester, and his employee," Luz Carmen said, the commanding tone was gone from her voice. "We need to let them help us, Andrés." The young man looked from her to Billy to me, the better eye focused for an extra beat on my face.

"You were the one in the pickup truck."

"Yeah, I'm the one," I said,—and couldn't help myself—"the one who saved your life."

WE ENDED UP outside. The reeking claustrophobia outweighed any need to keep Andrés Carmen out of sight. Billy and I sat on one side of the picnic table, the Carmens on the other.

The house trailer belonged to Andrés's girlfriend and her son, the teenager inside. Andrés had put his car in a storage garage on the other side of the airport where a friend of his did under-the-table auto work. He told us this as if he thought he was being slick. The thing that smart guys like him didn't realize is that cop work doesn't end like the sixty-minute police shows on TV. Real cops get paid by the hour, day after day. In a case like his, that be-on-the-lookout broadcast might stay on the daily rundown sheet for months, long after Andrés got desperate to use his car again.

Time was on the cop's side; watching out for punks and dealers and fuckups was their living. For 99 percent of the people they were after, criminal activity was their living. Eventually, the bad guys have to come out of their hole and go back to work. If they came out, they'd get caught. If they stayed in hiding, they wouldn't be committing their crimes. The cops won both ways.

Andrés's sneer of superiority lasted all of ten seconds.

"Who were the p-people trying to kill you?" Billy asked.

"They're just a bunch of dudes who have guns, you know," he said with a shrug.

"No, I don't, you know," Billy said, mocking the young man's use of the new mantra his generation seemed intent on injecting into every sentence. It was a usage Billy detested.

"What I do know is that your sister told you that the same car pulled up and fired several shots at her and Mr. Freeman in the park the other day, and you didn't seem to care that you'd put your sister in danger."

The brother averted his eyes. His hands were folded on top of the worn table. He started picking at the chipped paint with his fingernails. "She did that to herself," he finally said in a quieter tone.

"Andrés, I am trying to save you," Luz Carmen said.

It was the first time I'd heard a pleading tone in her voice.

"I told you this would happen, Andrés. I knew you would be caught and arrested. If they send you back to Bolivia now, you know you will not survive there, brother."

Another first: Luz Carmen began to cry.

"If you had not taken their business to this, this lawyer, there wouldn't be a problem, Luz. You didn't have to do that, you know. You could have said nothing, and I would still be making money."

Billy slammed his open palm down on the table: The actual shock of it made me jump. Any show of anger or frustration was so rare in the man that I was astounded, and speechless.

"Enough!" Billy snapped, and then went silent. His eyes had gone big, his face tight. It was hard for me to see my friend struggling to gain control. He had no practice at it. I could tell that he was biting the flesh inside his mouth when he stared again at Andrés Carmen, and without a hint of stutter demanded, "Who were the men in the Monte Carlo who were trying to kill you?"

Andrés looked at his sister, and then back at Billy.

"They call themselves Los Capos," he said. "They are like the enforcers, you know, from the old school of the street runners."

"Dealers?" Billy said.

"Sometimes," Andrés answered. "But mostly for a show of force, like in the old days."

"And what old days are we t-talking about here, Mr. Carmen?" Billy said, regaining his lawyerese as well as the stutter he'd temporarily lost in anger.

"You know, the drug hustling from when I was a little kid. You had a lot of the street work going on, the selling corners and the stash houses and all that," Andrés Carmen said. "With all those dudes running around, you had to have the guns and guys to keep people in line and enforce your areas. But that don't happen so much anymore." Andrés Carmen cut his eyes over at me.

"The cops shut a lot of that down. They got to a lot of people, and the money wasn't there anymore. Gangs started workin' out on one another. It got too dangerous."

I was thinking about the Brown Man, the former dealer I'd seen in front of the warehouse where our chase had begun.

"S-So how do these people become involved in a white-collar crime g-group swindling the federal government out of Medicare dollars?" Billy said, even though he knew the answer to the question.

"It's all about the money," Andrés Carmen said as though he was passing on a motivation he and his cohorts had just invented. "You make a lot more money with the Medicare stuff, and it isn't as dangerous as gettin' shot out on the corners, you know."

"At least, it was," Billy said, "you know?"

Andrés Carmen just shook his head and looked down at the tiny pile of paint chips he'd scraped together with his fingernails. We all remained quiet for a minute, sneaking looks at Billy, who was obviously now in control.

"OK, Andrés; this is wh-what I need from you. Put together as many names and descriptions of those people you've been working with as you can. Then I want l-locations, where you take the Medicare numbers and forms, where you've seen the computers and p-paperwork stored. I also want descriptions of the drugs you've seen at these locations b-because I already know that the police confiscated a trunk load from the Monte Carlo. If it's true that these p-people are employing your "old school" dealers, then they haven't given up that trade completely.

"You p-put all that together for me, and I will use it as leverage to try and keep you out of jail, and perhaps have some kind of influence with immigration if it comes to that."

Andrés did not say a word, but subtly nodded his head.

"If you run, you leave your s-sister in the wind, Andrés," Billy said to make his point. "If you b-believe that these enforcers are going to leave her alone once you're gone, you are wrong. And you're street-savvy enough to know you're wrong. In absence of you, they will go after her."

Still, Andrés said nothing.

"You know?" Billy repeated.

"Yeah," Andrés finally said. "I know."

12

WHEN I GOT home, Sherry was still at the office. Soon after her rehabilitation, she'd gone back part-time, but now she was an 8-to-5 woman, working cases from inside the Broward Sheriff's Office's corporate palace. It was mostly phone work, case evaluation, and meeting on occasion with crime victims. It was not what she was meant to do. She was the kind of cop who worked best on the outside, moving, watching, evaluating from the streets and the crime scenes. A lot of cops make the transition; after years on the streets, they move into the command structure, and behind a desk. Sherry's move was premature because of the leg, but she was pushing them on that.

The victim advocacy thing was a step. Several times, she'd gone out to meet with the victims and their families in her capacity as a detective. The guys who caught the case weren't always happy with what they considered her horning in on their investigations, but she'd played it carefully: "Only here to help with the social stuff, fellas. I'm not taking anything from you, and any intel I get goes straight to your ears only."

I knew it was a step back for her. She'd worked long and hard to get her detective's shield, and hated the idea of playing second fiddle to the others. Every time I told her she'd get it back, she just nodded. "Yeah, I know, Max. I just have to work harder now, right?"

In the kitchen, I rooted through the refrigerator and came up with salami and provolone on wheat bread for lunch. I popped the top of the last beer and went out onto the patio and sat in one of the lounge chairs next to the pool. Under the big oak, there was enough shade to take off the heat of the day. While I stared at the pool water, I ran the trailer park scenario through my head again.

At the end of our picnic table discussion, Billy laid down the law to Andrés, who assured him that the enforcers he'd told us about had no knowledge of his girlfriend's home. Billy and I both knew that the criminal grapevine would lead there eventually. Some guy would ask some guy who would know Andrés's girlfriend, or a girlfriend who knew his girlfriend, and they would track the location down.

I offered to let Andrés hide out at my shack in the Glades. My quick description of the place seemed to the scare the shit out of the kid, but Billy convinced me that ethically we didn't want to get in the business of trying to hide him from the authorities.

Instead, Billy left him with orders: "Don't use your car and stay put right here until I get in touch with you. That's for your sake, and your sister's."

Luz Carmen was another matter. After leaving Andrés, we took her home to pack up enough belongings to last a week. While the two of them were inside, I drove Billy's car around the neighborhood, watching for any kind of surveillance by either the so-called enforcers or the now-alerted cops. We doubted whether the sheriff's office would jump on an investigation so quickly, but Billy didn't want to take a chance.

When Luz was packed and ready to go, we drove south to Deerfield Beach, where Billy had a safe house on the sand where he kept out-of-state clients or witnesses when trial dates were close. The Royal Flamingo Villas was a perfect, low-key, unobtrusive collection of one- and two-room bungalows that straddled either side of A1A. Billy's place was given to him as payment by a client whose ass he'd saved in a lawsuit. The small stucco building sat directly on the oceanfront, out of sight to any traffic. Luz Carmen objected the entire trip to the house until she saw the accommodations, and then agreed: "Yes, this will work."

When we got back to Billy's, I told him that I would rent a car while my truck was being fixed so I could take the descriptions of the dealers Andrés had given us, and do some tracking. Billy just winked at me as we pulled into the parking area of his building.

"Already t-taken care of," he said. "I m-made a call while we were at Luz Carmen's house." He stopped his Lexus in the outside parking lot in front of a glossy black 1989 Plymouth Gran Fury and tossed me a key ring.

"It's the p-police pursuit model," he said. "The client who gave it to me p-put a 360, four-barrel engine in when he restored it. I'm told it is very fast, and very heavy, and can take quite a b-beating without doing damage to the occupant."

I just looked at him in amazement, and then got out, walking around the Gran Fury like a kid seeing his first Hot Wheels. It was vintage, replete with the old police black-wall tires and small hubcaps. The spotlights were still mounted in front of the side windows, a handle and trigger on the inside. I opened the driver-side door and got in. The interior was pristine and had even been sprayed with that stuff that gave it the smell of new carpet and vinyl. I hit the ignition and felt the rumble as much as heard it when I gassed the motor. When I looked up, Billy had already gone—no doubt with a smile on his face.

WAITING FOR SHERRY to come home, I had the same stupid smile on my face, as I imagined her seeing the Gran Fury sitting in her driveway.

While I sat poolside, I sipped a beer and took out my copy of the list of names and descriptions of the men Andrés had met, and the menu of drugs he'd seen at the warehouse. When I'd asked him who the man was who greeted him outside the warehouse before our chase began, Andrés told me, "That was Carlyle. They call him Brown."

"Carlyle" was the real name of the Brown Man. A few years back, he'd been running a lucrative drug corner in Northwest Fort Lauderdale. I'd run into him trying to find the notorious Eddie the Junkman, the ghostly but all too real serial killer Sherry had saved me from by putting a bullet in his head. Eddie was a mentally challenged drug user who roamed the neighborhood in the guise of being homeless.

He had needs, the most prevalent being sex and drugs. Prostitutes and young women in his hunting area had learned to turn down his sexual advances after he shared his crack cocaine with them. But Eddie had learned, too.

A huge and thickly muscled man, he entrapped the women with his bulk, then put a broad hand over their mouths while he satisfied his sexual needs. The fact that the women suffocated in the process did not bother him. During Billy's and my investigation of elderly women being similarly suffocated in a life insurance scam gone ugly, I'd swung a deal with the Brown Man. He'd given up Eddie for the exchange of his own business survival. It was time I revisited Carlyle.

Considering the foot dragging of any governmental agency like the sheriff's office, Hammonds's investigators would move slowly on the warehouse address. I might get a chance at the Brown Man before they spooked him.

The other names Andrés had given us were probably a.k.a.'s as well. There were two guys known as the Marlin brothers, who may or may not be brothers at all; a so-called supervisor known as Anthony Monroe; and a computer tech everyone called Joey "the code writer" Porter. According to Andrés, Carlyle was the man who did most of the drug movement, a line of products considered a sideline by the others, who seemed to tolerate it, but kept their hands off unless there was some reason to party—like when some big government check came in, and everyone was flush.

When asked to list the drugs, Andrés had written down mostly prescription drugs like painkillers: oxycodone and Percocet, over-the-counter amphetamines like Dexedrine and Adderall, and opiates like buprenophine, as well as boxes of Xanax and anabolic steroids.

Though the kid's spelling was atrocious, Billy had been impressed by Andrés's recall of the supply. The kid simply said, "I keep my eyes down when I'm in there, like I don't want to know nothing, or I'm afraid to look them in the eye. Instead I'm looking at the boxes, you know, the labels and stuff. They pay me to do what I do, not to know what I know."

I'd asked him if he knew where the drugs went after they left the warehouse. "I don't do drugs. I don't know nothing about them, man," he said, lifting his chin, as if this was a point of pride for him. "My money ain't drug money."

Billy's face had tightened as he'd read through the list of drugs. He knew that every one of them had been on the A-list of adolescent abused prescription drugs for years. "Feeding the children," he'd simply said, staring into Andrés's eyes.

Andrés put his head down, eyes again on the tabletop. "I don't use them, you know."

It was the mantra of every low-level drug runner I'd ever arrested or known: Take the money and don't get involved. Get what you can, do what you're told, and don't be ambitious.

It's ambition that gets the runners and couriers and corner boys shot, left for dead in an alley after they'd try to skim or short, or peddle a little on their own. Andrés probably wasn't ambitious. He probably never put his fingers on the real money in an operation like this. But his sister's dreams for him had put him in someone's gun sights now.

The list of drugs somehow made sense: The Medicare scam had to touch the medical community—doctors' offices, pharmacies, nursing homes—at least on the edges. Hell, Billy had pulled up a story that showed how a hospital in California had been running a similar billing scam, bringing in "patients" off the street, and then billing for expensive equipment and testing that was never used or done. It would not be too slippery a slope to find out that someone also had their fingers in the prescription drug till.

I was running the possibilities through my head when I heard the jiggling of the gate door leading in from the drive. After a few seconds, I heard the door clack shut, the familiar sound of Sherry returning from a day at the office. She rolled in dressed in her business attire: a conservative short-sleeved blouse and a dark skirt. She had adamantly stated while still in rehab that she would never wear a "pinned-up pair of pants" in public. If she wanted to show her incredibly taut and muscled single leg, she would.

"Let them use their imagination," she'd said. "I don't give a shit."

I greeted her as she made it up the ramp.

"Hi."

"Hey," she said. "I thought you were going to be with Billy all day."

"Didn't take that long," I said. "We found the sister and her brother. Made sure the sister was safe, and Billy's going to see if he can put some leverage together to get the feds in on busting the Medicare scam and get her into a protection program while they do it."

I gave her a quick rundown on the case. Sherry and I tried not to get too deep into the ongoing investigations in which each of us was involved. It could get dicey sometimes.

"And was that car sitting in my driveway any kind of recompense for making a deal with the brother," she said, a playful look in her eyes, one that I rarely saw these days.

"Uh, nope, that would be the loaner that Billy gave me while the truck is being fixed," I said, unable to keep from matching her smile.

"Nice. Reminds me of my daddy's old prowl car," she said and rolled up next to me in the wheelchair. "I like the side lights. I used to hear old stories of the boys spotlighting deer along the roadside with those things up in Apopka."

Sherry rarely talked about her family. Her father had been an old-time sheriff up in Central Florida. She called herself an original Florida cracker, born and raised in an area that thirty years ago was more open field and cattle range than the Disney World spillover it now represents.

"Those old spotlights would catch the deer right in the eyes, and they'd freeze up like statues—easy killing."

"Cheating," I said. Spotting game was illegal throughout most of the country. Some considered it an unfair advantage. But then the same folks thought nothing of feeding deer for eleven months out of the year under a tree stand. Then on the first legal day of hunting season, they'll sit up there with a high-powered rifle and blast away—fish in a barrel. I could never see the challenge in it.

"You didn't personally know any of these spotters?" I said.

"Considering who my daddy was, I probably kissed one every night after the family dinner," she said, looking out into the light of the pool. "The law gets interpreted in different ways, even by lawmen."

There was something on her mind and it didn't have anything to do with deer hunting. She finally looked over at me and asked, "Could you get me a beer?"

"Sure," I said, getting up and kissing her on the forehead as I headed for the kitchen.

When I got back with two cold beers, Sherry had gotten out of her wheelchair and moved to the side of the pool. Her foot was in the water, lazily kicking up a soft boil. Her stump was on the edge. It looked uncomfortable, but I suppressed the urge to ask if she wanted a cushion or pillow to put underneath. If she wanted that, she'd ask.

I sat down on the deck behind her, looking in the opposite direction, and matched up my back to hers, and leaned into it. I felt her give her weight back into mine, and we adjusted the balance until it was just so.

"So what did you find out?" I asked.

"About?" was her answer.

"Booker."

I felt her head turn just a bit.

"Did I tell you I was going to look into him?"

"No. But you did."

"You know me too well, Max."

"I try."

I heard the plop of her foot when she brought it up and let it splash back into the water. I felt a chuckle in her chest ripple and vibrate into my own. I liked the feel of her laughter.

"I pulled the files on his accident, both the initial reports, and the investigative sheets afterward." Her voice was careful. I knew her well enough to know that this was an effort to be unbiased. Just the fact that she'd started out using that voice let me know it would soon change.

"The woman he was pulling over was a seventy-eight-year-old retiree from Sunrise. When the car rear-ended her, she suffered a whiplash, broken nose, and lacerations from her face ramming the steering wheel on the rebound. She was nearly unconscious when the paramedics got there. She never saw a thing."

"OK," I said, letting her start wherever she wanted.

"Her ID and ownership of the car all checked out. She told the investigators she was going to pick up her granddaughter at the airport. That checked out, too.

"The car that hit them was stolen. The owner, some old fiberglass marine worker from Sailboat Bend in Fort Lauderdale, didn't even know the car had been stolen until the deputies got to his place and woke him up at eight the next morning. He was sleeping with his sixty-three-year-old girlfriend, who said they'd been in bed together all night.

"The guy volunteered to take a blood test for alcohol or drugs or whatever they wanted. The deputies noted that he seemed to be legitimately saddened when they told him what had happened. He didn't even ask about the car. They checked out his story anyway, and found out he'd worked for the same yacht builder on the New River for more than thirty years, and did old-time car restoration on the side."

Now Sherry's voice was picking up, in both emotion and volume.

"When the crime scene guys had the car towed in, they went over the thing with a fine-tooth comb. Found nothing useful—pristine inside. All surfaces wiped clean, no inconsistent fibers: There was nothing inside that didn't belong to the owner. Clean."

"Too clean," I said.

"Way too clean," Sherry said, and I felt her back shift again.

"So the crime scene guys didn't find a laundry ticket on the floor belonging to an ex-con car thief, or a soda can in the cup holder with his DNA spit on the side, or a lock of blonde hair with a one-of-a-kind conditioner sold at only one salon in the country?"

I felt Sherry's head shake back and forth. She knew my predisposition to bitch about the public's expectation that criminal investigations actually mirror the bullshit they see on television. But I agreed: This wasn't the time or place.

"Sorry," I said. She took a minute and a long swallow of beer before continuing.

"I can see a party-time car thief racing down I-595 and rear-ending a parked car; but what kind of guy sees that he's pinched a cop off at the knees, and then takes the time to carefully wipe down the inside of the car before he books on foot?"

"Someone who isn't just partying; someone who is very cool in an emergency," I said. "A pro who does the car thing for a living—a guy who knows how to handle himself when shit goes wrong."

"That's some cool customer to be thinking of that while a cop is a hood ornament, screaming and squirting blood all over your car."

"Jesus," I said, the vision actually making me shudder. She must have felt it through her back.

"Sorry," she said.

We took a sip of beer at the same time, our heads lightly thumping together as we both went back to swallow. The slight collision made us both laugh.

"Hard head," she said.

"Pot calling the kettle," I said, and then added, "so what did you get when you went to internal affairs?"

This time I felt her turn, and knew she was looking at the side of my face.

"You're starting to scare me, Max," she said with a hint of fun, but also a bit of seriousness in her voice.

"Well, if you start to entertain the thought that Booker might have been the target of a pro, you have to find out why some ruthless son of a bitch would do such a thing, right?"

"IA wouldn't give me anything," Sherry said. "They wouldn't say whether somebody he'd busted had a grudge for Booker, or that he'd gotten any threatening messages—nothing. They stonewalled me completely. So I had to go over their heads to a source."

This was the line in our respective work that didn't get crossed. I wasn't going to ask who she used as a source in the department. But I knew that a law enforcement organization is no different that any other office enterprise. People talk. It's a human trait you don't give up just because you're told to. Civilization demands it. Societal living depends on it. It is why I do not believe in government conspiracies. Someone always spills eventually.

"So?"

Sherry waited, assessing whether she was talking out of school.

"The skeleton is in their closet," she finally said. "The word is that Booker had steroids in his blood system, and that they found elevated levels of caffeine during a tox screen at the hospital. They kept it out of the media and off the books so he could get the maximum coverage for his disability payout."

"A lifter doing Red Bull," I said.

"The guy was hurt enough losing his legs, Max. They didn't want to hurt him more by putting an illegal-steroid-use sheet in his file, and having that put his health coverage in jeopardy."

The guy was hurt enough? Even if she was talking about someone else, it would be the first time Sherry admitted that losing a leg was a devastating thing. I thought about a Robert Frost quote: "Tell other people's stories as if they happened to you, and tell your own as if they happened to other people."

We sat in silence awhile. Was burying the steroid use an act of compassion by the sheriff's office? Did you let an infraction of the steroid ban screw up Booker's life more than it already was?

"So does he feel beholden to the department, or to his buddies?" I finally said, talking out loud more than anything else. It didn't take a genius to figure that if Booker was doing steroids, then his buddies at the gym either knew it, or where into it themselves.

I heard Sherry's foot plop a few more times in the pool, could feel her hip working against mine.

"Not sure," she said. "But I'm going to have lunch with him again tomorrow. I know there's a lot in his head he's not giving up. Maybe he needs a release."

As do you, my love, I thought, but didn't say it out loud.

13

THE NEXT DAY, I followed the Brown Man home. I'd parked the Gran Fury in the warehouse parking lot, where I could watch the front door of BioMechanics Inc., and had not been disappointed. The Escalade that had been there the day before was in place when I arrived at 9:00 in the morning.

Billy had tracked the license plates of the Mercedes and the big SUV on his computers. A company name came up as the owner of the Mercedes, and Billy was running it further. But the Escalade was registered to a Charles Coombs in northwest Fort Lauderdale.

By doing a comparison search of previous arrest records on Carlyle Carter, a.k.a. the Brown Man, the name *Coombs* also appeared. Coombs was listed as both an associate and as a defense witness on an aggravated assault charge filed against Carlyle that never made it to court. He might be a cousin or just a neighborhood friend of the Brown Man, but a better guess was they were running buddies who swapped identities and registered properties.

Putting things you owned in someone else's name was a way of getting around seizures and liens, and making claims of indigence when you got caught in the system. But you better trust the one whose name you use. When Carlyle "the Brown Man" Carter came out of the warehouse at 1:00 P.M. and climbed into the driver's seat of the Escalade, it didn't matter whose name was on the papers: He was mine.

Again the tail led me south on State Road 7. When I recognized two or three intersections I'd barreled through just two days ago, the recollection made my hands involuntarily tighten on the steering wheel. But I was riding in a different style today, rolling in the classic Gran Fury, the old-time suspension feeling softer than that in my pickup, but the engine sounding more powerful and quietly strong. I thought about the pit bull at Andrés's hideout. When I pressed the accelerator, it was like walking a dangerous dog with a heavy leash; the engine pulled at you to let it run, and you could feel the muscle behind it.

Easy boy, I whispered. I realized there was a macho pride in driving such a machine, but the lack of recognition or even a second look by the daytime traffic around me tempered the thought. No one in this day and age gave a shit.

The Brown Man took me all the way south through Lauderhill before turning east. I watched for addresses. He was heading straight to the house listed as belonging to Mr. Coombs. The fact that Carlyle was taking a direct route was both curious and unsettling. He didn't seem to give a damn if anyone followed him despite the hit attempt on one of his minions, or even a fellow employee—whichever Andrés was. Carlyle seemed unconcerned, which would mean he either ordered it, or knew nothing about it.

Still, I kept a block and a half back as he turned into a neighborhood of single-story stucco homes, most of which looked like they came out of a 1960s cookie-cutter mold in the days when South Florida sprawl was rolling west as fast as man and machine could drain the swamp and slap down concrete slabs for people to live on. Carlyle was driving slowly—no hurry and seemingly no worry.

The homes on the street were a mishmash of living styles, if not architecture. Three houses in a row had dirt for yards, old-time jalousie windows, and carports stacked with old boxes and furniture and assorted junk. Then, all of a sudden, an immaculately kept residence with a green manicured lawn, freshly painted shutters, and flowerbeds overflowing with bright-colored bougainvillea would appear. There was a place with a chain-link fence surrounding every inch of some owner's property. Then another rattrap, then a modest but clean home next door. No one was on the street at midday. This was not where drugs would be sold on the corner, not a hangout for yellow-eyed men to slump in their despair. The homes here stood quietly and said "working class."

I watched as the Brown Man turned the next corner. His brake lights flashed. I used a boxlike ficus hedge as a shield and eased forward to watch the Escalade slow and then ease into a driveway guarded by an eight-foot-high metal fence. A gated entry was rolling back, probably triggered by Carlyle from his SUV, and he pulled in and parked on a broad concrete lot. Compared to the surroundings, the house was a palace, two stories with wide sun-reflecting one-way windows. The entire place was painted bright white and had a full barrel-tile roof in pink and terra-cotta tones.

Behind the ostentatious structure, I could see a three-story screen attached to the back indicating an outdoor pool and patio. You saw these kinds of homes along the Intracoastal Waterway and in the rich suburbs of Coral Springs, but not in the modest neighborhoods of Northwest Fort Lauderdale. The Brown Man had made his money and made no bones about it. The tax man, the policeman, the competition be damned. Here I am, the drug dealer was saying: Catch me if you can.

I watched Carlyle get out of the SUV and walk through the double front doors of the house. He glanced back once, watching, I assumed, to make sure that the now closing gate was rolling appropriately shut. Since I was still blocking a stop sign, I turned onto the street, and settled in the shade of one of the few large trees on the block.

Well, crime pays, I thought, turning off the engine of the Gran Fury.

Carlyle was about my age. Six years ago, he was sitting on a stool in a prime drug market, selling crack to strung-out hookers, and ratting out a warped serial killer whose penchant for choking his sex partners to death had brought too much scrutiny to the Brown Man's turf. Had his profitable drug business bought him this ostentatious lifestyle? Or did his jump into Medicare fraud enrich him? Billy's record check had shown the house that sat on this double corner lot was supposedly purchased in 2004 under the Coombs's name. Renovation licensing had been signed for by Coombs. But the way Carlyle had walked into the place, with that air of ownership, I had no doubt it was his.

Maybe Mr. Carter is simply a very prosperous businessman, I told myself. But even the unspoken words in my head made me say out loud, "Bullshit."

I sat for fifteen minutes, maybe twenty, marking details: the tall white metallic fence that appeared to completely surround the property, the surveillance cameras mounted in obvious positions at the gate and on the garage doors, the basketball hoop with a Plexiglas backboard on the wide parking area, a nice touch. I wondered what the inside of the place might be like.

I was actually playing with the idea of simply walking up and requesting an interview when the front doors opened, and Carlyle and a boy of about nine or ten stepped out. Both of them were looking directly at me.

I fidgeted, felt myself unconsciously shift in my seat, and watched them walk to the gate as it rolled open. Carlyle was dressed as he had been when he'd entered, in an open-collared silk shirt and dress slacks. The boy was in knee-length shorts and a simple blue polo shirt, almost like a relaxed school uniform.

As they walked directly toward me, the former drug dealer's face was placid and expressionless. I watched his hands, which were empty and out front. There were no lumps that would indicate weapons, though I could not see the small of his back. When they were thirty feet away, their destination obvious, Carlyle seemed to read my mind, and raised his arms above his head and did a little pirouette, playfully, but purposely causing his shirt to rise above his waistline to show he was unarmed. The boy, whose complexion and shape was a miniature of the man, sported a smile and an excited look.

I opened the driver-side door and stepped out as they approached.

"Wow," said the kid, not looking at me, focused on the car. "Nice car, man." The boy's face could not hide his honest thrill as he stepped up to the front of the Gran Fury and looked at his reflection in the polished surface of the black hood.

The Brown Man had his hand out, extending it to me as if we were old friends or acquaintances meeting on a pleasant sunny afternoon.

"Good day, sir," he said, with a lilt in his voice I knew had not been there when I first encountered him working the streets.

I stepped forward and took his hand, giving a single pump, and then withdrawing it.

"Hello, Carlyle," I said.

The man's eyes narrowed as he put an extra effort into looking at my face. "No one uses that name for me," he said. His tone was moderated, not with surprise, or disapproval, or threat. "Do I know you, sir?"

"We've met in the past. Over a mutual, uh, concern," I said. "My name is Max Freeman."

He continued to search my face. "My apologies, sir. Perhaps you were in uniform before? I've met many people in uniform."

I watched the Brown Man's eyes cutting behind me. I half-turned to see the boy now peering in the window of the Gran Fury, with that same "ooh, ahh" look on his face. He ran his hand over the chrome egg of the side-mounted spotlight, and then quickly used the tail of his shirt to polish off his fingerprints.

"No," I said, turning back. "Our mutual acquaintance was a homeless junk man with some very bad habits."

As the Brown Man raised his brow, a light of recognition slipped into his eyes.

"Ah, the PI," he said, and then shook his head as if remembering. "A nasty business, yes?"

"Eddie the Junk Man," I said.

"A beast of a man."

"A dead beast," I said, holding eye contact with the drug dealer a bit longer than I meant to.

The Brown Man looked beyond me.

"My son has a fascination with classic cars," he said. "Right, Andrew?"

The boy was still enthralled.

"It's a Plymouth, right?" he said to me.

"Yes," I said, talking to him over the shimmer of the polished roof. "A 1975 Gran Fury. They were mostly used as police cars back in the day."

The boy moved to the passenger-side window and cupped his face with his hands to reduce the glare as he peered inside.

"Go ahead. Open the door," I said. "Take a look inside."

The boy's eyes lit up at the suggestion, but he looked to his father first to get the man's approval. Carlyle nodded, and the boy opened the door and climbed in.

"Information out on the streets is that you've gone into a new line of business, Carlyle," I said, figuring, what the hell: Sometimes you have to ask the hard questions first and sort through the bullshit. He did not turn his eyes from the windshield of my car, where he could watch his son through the glass.

"As an entrepreneur, Mr. Free-Man," he said, putting an emphasis on both syllables of my last name. "I have business dealings in lots of areas, mostly as an investor."

He smiled, showing brilliant white teeth. Whether he was smiling at his son's fascination or at my insouciance was up to interpretation.

"This particular arena of business would be Medicare fraud, Mr. Brown Man," I said.

My use of his old street name caused a twitch in his stoic and professional demeanor. He gave me no response.

"The family member of another player in this, ah, investment opportunity of yours has become a target. She's a bystander, an innocent. She was shot at while I was with her. Which means I was shot at—which I don't like."

Carlyle Carter put his hands behind his back. His eyes still did not meet mine.

"You know my past, Mr. Free-Man. You know what I did, and I ain't gonna deny it," he said, losing some of his white-collar business speak.

"But times have changed. The product has changed. The people done changed and the demand changed. But addiction don't change.

Another generation comes in, their taste is different—but that urge won't dry up, Free-Man."

I clasped my hands in front of me, the opposite profile of Carlyle, but I turned to gaze through the windshield just as he had as he watched his son.

"I do recall that a substantial supply of steroids and amphetamines and other prescription drugs were found in the trunk of a recently wrecked gangbanger's car," I said, tossing more out there.

"See? There you go," Carlyle said.

"And that kind of product would be your area of expertise."

I felt the man shrug more than saw it.

"A mature man don't sell the streets no more like some beggar," he said, a tick of frustration now in his voice. "Them young boys? They're tryin' to get the thrills because they've heard stories of the old days. They'll do almost anything, so you're best not to mess with them. Nowadays, a smart man deals only with people he knows, people he trusts—people of a certain position, who can cover your ass, Mr. Free-Man—you know?"

I could feel Carlyle Carter's eyes on the side of my face when he said the words, making it personal instead of rhetorical. I looked at him as he signaled his son with a crooked finger. Before the boy got out, Carlyle made one last statement.

"I got nothin' to do with no shootin' Mr. Free-Man. Ya'll do guns. The young bloods do guns. I got responsibilities now, man," he said, nodding at his son. "I don't do guns. I've got nothin' to do with it."

Carlyle turned and started back to his gated house. The boy caught up, but turned to me and waved.

"Thanks, mister. That's a cool ride."

14

Sittin' here restin' my bones

Where the hell did that old Otis Redding tune come from? Man, that's like one of those ancient ones Dad would have been playing in the garage while he was working on one of those old junkers of his. The old man always had his head under the hood of some falling apart Oldsmobile 98, or a salvaged Caddy with a sprung rear bumper and peeling landau roof. Smell of gasoline in your nose since you were old enough to toddle out to the garage and search him out. Big door open to the big world, sun streaming in through the dust particles while your father teaches you the sizes of socket wrenches and spark plug gaps. Good old days.

Shit, you're losin' it, Booker. Fucking good mood you're in going all nostalgic and shit, eh?

Yeah, OK, admit it, it is nice sittin' here in the sun and watching the beach and waiting for a good-looking athletic woman coming to meet you for lunch. And she's a wheelie and a cop, just like you.

Well, not exactly like you. She at least has her shit together a little. She went back to her job. She's doing her sheriff's office work even if it is on the inside. How long would it take for you to ever make it on the inside, man? Riding a desk? No fucking way. You're a street man—always have been, right?

Well, look at yourself now, dude. You're just veggin'. Existing like a fucking tomato. Admit it, what do you have? It's not like you can keep on pumpin' over at the gym and your legs are going to grow back.

OK, don't go all negative now, man, and screw up the lunch. Take another Vicodin and chill. As long as you can still keep the pain down and be a stand-up guy you've got something, right? Hah! Stand up—nice joke, Marty. Maybe you can use that one on her.

Yeah, you're stand up, all right, staying true to those guys at the gym even though they won't have a fucking thing to do with you anymore. What, you lose your quads and they kick you to the street? I don't need their fucking steroids anymore. Yeah, they can still get me the pain meds, as much as I want. But I oughta rat those fuckers out on this drug thing. I can get the scripts from the rehab doc just as easily now.

Hell, you were gettin' close to doing that anyway, weren't you? Well, maybe, but there were some good times with those guys. That gig you did with Jesse Holshouser when you were both third-year patrol and went charging into that burning house to get the lady out. That was pretty cool. Hell, we didn't even think about it, just did what first responders are supposed to do. Everybody high-fivin' us after that one, like heroes, right? The old man would've liked that one, right? Doin' it the way your dad wanted you to do it, makin' him proud.

Still, it wasn't long after that when the gang really started up at the gym. Guys pumpin' up, feeling good about being strong and stronger. Maybe it was just a competition thing.

Admit it, it was kinda sweet that these guys were so hungry not just for the steroids to get all pumped up, but also the oxy and the Dexedrine and Adderall—and we were the ones who had it.

Then comes McKenzie: The guy was turning it into some kind of business, supplying everybody in the gym, whether they were fellow cops or not. Shit, we all didn't mind going along with it as long as he was just sharing it with other officers from our jurisdiction, guys you could trust, because they were really layin' their own asses and careers on the line. But fucking McKenzie was starting to sell it to his bar bouncer buddies and guys from other departments—and that was just stupid.

You knew it was getting crazy, Marty. But shit, get it out of your head man, 'cause here comes the detective now. And whoa, look at her, with her blonde hair blowin' in the breeze. She's crankin' that chair.

Look, even the walking guys are checking her out. Man, those triceps are cut. No wonder she kicked McKenzie's ass on those dips.

Look at her, Marty: This chick is way confident. How the hell does she do that, man? I need to get that back. I need to be proud of myself again.

15

SHERRY MET ME for dinner at Lester's because I like the meat loaf with real mashed potatoes, and I think she likes putting her chin up and overpowering the handicap ramp that climbs at a ridiculous angle because it's grandfathered-in and thus legal. It's her statement: Make it difficult, I'm coming in anyway.

I also like the old-style diner for its monster-size coffee cups and the vinyl-covered booths that afford at least a little privacy when you're talking shop. Lester's used to be a hangout for sheriff's deputies and Fort Lauderdale cops on coffee breaks, but that changed after the sheriff's office moved to its Broward Boulevard palace years ago. The addition of I-595 effectively detoured the truckers who used to frequent the place. But the joint is still quaint and familiar, especially if you like gum-cracking waitresses who call you "hon." You can also trust that there will be a tiny tin pitcher of real cream on your table instead of those infernal little peel-n-pour thimbles of who knows what.

I was still sipping my first bowl of coffee—the sixteen-ounce porcelain one with the faded blue stripe around the rim—and taking my time to respond to Sherry's bomb of a theory.

"Maybe the car wreck wasn't an accident. Maybe somebody tried to kill him."

"OK," I said, swallowing, and running the statement through my head while the warm caffeine was hitting my brain. "Where the hell did that possibility come from?"

"The guy opened up to me a little," Sherry said, her fingers pushing a napkin around on the table in front of her. We sat in a booth in the far corner of the dining area. Sherry had pulled alongside, and then slid herself into the opposite side to face me, the side that would allow her words to be absorbed by the wall behind me.

"This on the second time you've had lunch with a legless man who wouldn't talk to any of his professional therapists and shrinks?"

"Yeah," she said, putting that little smile on the corner of her mouth. "I'm pretty good."

"I agree with half of that statement," I said. "You are pretty."

She smirked.

"You've always been a jealous man, Max."

"Agreed," I said, and took another sip of coffee. "So lay out the theory, Detective. I mean, I'm guessing it isn't an official case yet, right?"

She looked up at me as if she thought I was being smart-assed about the statement, but I wasn't.

"Booker says that the group at the gym was pretty much into the whole steroid thing. They'd started it just wanting to see what it could do, and then it blossomed on them—some sort of competitive thing he couldn't really enunciate."

"Yeah, well, the steroids were pretty apparent by the acne all over that McKenzie guy's neck and shoulders," I said.

Sherry chuckled. "And you didn't even see the way his face turned purple when he was trying to beat me at the dips—definite high blood pressure syndrome. Anyway, they started out small-time. But pretty soon, everybody in the core group was on board."

The waitress came to our booth, cracked her gum, and refilled my cup with the glass orb of coffee that seemed to be locked into the hand of every server in the place. I ordered the meat loaf and Sherry got chopped salad, uh, without the ham, please, and can you take the yolk out of the boiled egg, uh, and no onions and just oil and vinegar dressing, thanks.

The waitress smiled a perturbed smile. Sherry gave her that fake "too bad I'm the customer and you're not" look. I shook my head and kept my mouth shut as the she gathered the menus and left.

"Booker told you all this?" I said.

"Yeah."

"Why?"

"I think he trusts me. I told him I had nothing to do with IA, and that it was the behavioral unit that asked me to meet him. I told him they never said anything about a drug use problem. And anyway, I wasn't the one who brought it up to begin with."

"He offered to talk about drugs?"

"Yeah, sort of."

"Sort of?"

"Well, I did say that I'd done some digging on his case. I told him the stuff about the clean car, the wiped-down clean car, and how weird that seemed."

"And?"

"He agreed. That's what they told him every time he tried to check on the status of the investigation of the hit-and-run driver who pinned him. They always told him they didn't have any leads. Even he was smart enough to wonder what the hell was going on."

"And the drugs?" I said, looking directly into Sherry's eyes.

"Well, that brought me to the blood tox report that I'd seen off the record—which led to the steroid discussion."

"That's not sort of," I said.

Sherry just shrugged.

"So he didn't have much of a chance to deny the steroids after you told him IA already had that," I said, and took another full swallow of coffee.

"He actually seemed contrite," Sherry said. "It was like he didn't want me to think badly of him. He tells me the stuff about the gym group and then says he was trying to distance himself anyway, trying to cut back on his use. He talked about getting older and more mature and how it's a young man's game out there—all that shit."

I was happy to hear her use that little invective at the end. She was making the guy out to be not such an asshole. Maybe I was feeling jealous.

"So he spills about the group doing the drugs, how does that tie into him being crushed on purpose?" I said, trying to stay on track.

"It's just speculation, Max. Don't look at me like that," Sherry said. Her oddly defensive position was rescued by the arrival of our food. I knew she'd continue when she was ready, not before.

I speared off chunks of the thick meat loaf, dipped them into the mashed potatoes and gravy, and then forked the whole mess into my mouth. I knew she was watching. She hated when I did that. But I had an ex-wife in Philly who'd been as controlling as anyone I'd met besides my father. The woman had gone on to climb the police administration ladder while I'd stuck with patrol—one of the reasons for our divorce. I'd sworn never to try to change myself again to please someone else's vision. Sherry accepted that, but maybe I pushed my "I'm gonna do it the way I want to do it" thing a little too far.

"Anyway," she started in again, "Booker says that in the early days he was the one designated to take delivery of the steroids, supposedly because he was on the night shift, and they could make the exchange in the dark, and no one would question it."

I nodded, my mouth full. At least I wasn't that uncouth.

"Obviously, he counts the stuff out, makes sure the payment is right," Sherry said.

"OK."

"After a while, additional stuff starts getting tossed in with the 'roids, painkillers, and the prescription shit," she said. "Booker says he started bitching about being a mule, and told the others he wasn't comfortable doing the gig anymore."

I left my green beans untouched and pushed my plate away.

I didn't have to say anything to Sherry about the confluence of what Booker was talking about, and the stuff Andrés Carmen had detailed from his visits to the Medicare scam warehouse. But neither one of us was going to make the leap to connect the two. As Billy said, the prescription drug market was expanding all of the time, and here in South Florida, anything that was happening across the nation was happening at an accelerated rate in Miami, Fort Lauderdale, Boca Raton, and the Keys.

We had the perfect storm of unadulterated glitz and high living, historical black markets that went back a hundred years to the rum-running days, rampant drug crime fueled over the last fifty years by smugglers from nearby South American growers, and an international culture of backroom bargaining and payoffs. If the illegal buying-and-selling of prescription drugs was the newest game in town, there'd be plenty of it going on here, with multitudes of players sticking their fingers in it.

Neither of us was going to bring up the possible coincidence that the group Billy and I had stumbled onto was a supplier to a group of steroid-using cops. At least, not yet. We are detectives. We don't do coincidence.

"So let me guess," I said. "When Booker starts getting cold feet over the whole drug thing, they don't just let him walk away."

"He doesn't ask to," Sherry said. "It's his group, Max, his identity. He said he was giving up the drugs, but according to him, that's when the others started losing trust in him. He says they definitely got nervous, started treating him differently."

"So you think the group got so paranoid that they decided to hit one of their own to keep him from ratting them out?" The tone of my voice must have been incredulous enough to piss her off.

"I didn't come up with it, Max. Booker did. He's the one who threw the possibility out there. He says that the guys started moving away from him, finding different machines to work when he was in the gym, stopped inviting him along to Dolphins games, and didn't have him over to their homes for parties like before."

"And this was before the accident?"

"Yeah, and now they've shut him out completely."

The waitress came and cleared the table and filled my cup.

"So let me guess which of these lifters was taking the orders and handling the money before it went over to Booker," I finally said, already guessing at the answer.

"You got it," Sherry shook her head. "McKenzie. Why is it that the mouthiest, yappiest dog in the kennel is the one they put in charge?"

"Every gang has its lead mutt," I said. "The rest like to come in after it takes the first bite."

I looked over the rim of my cup and noticed that Sherry was shifting in her seat, subtly rocking her weight from hip to hip. She was anxious and fidgety.

"Are you going to check McKenzie's IA file?" I said, taking a stab at what she might be thinking.

"I could do that. But it would have to be handled carefully," she said, catching me watching her. "For some reason, I don't want to blow this guy's trust."

"Booker?"

"Yeah, he's obviously coming out. Telling me all this is a big step for him, Max. If he thinks I'm just using him for some internal steroid investigation bullshit, he'll shut down again, and never trust anyone."

I just nodded, tried not to see the questions that started popping up in my head. Sherry was concerned about some stranger shutting down, when she herself had never completely opened up about her own feelings about her amputation. Maybe this guy Booker was the mirror she'd refused to look into. Maybe if I just let it go, she'd see her own reflection in there, and we could all move on.

Leaving a hefty tip and a wink to the waitress, we left for the parking lot. The old Gran Fury had a big enough trunk to easily fit Sherry's wheelchair. I was just hitting the ignition when my cell rang.

"Max, I apologize for the lateness of the call," Billy said.

"Yes?"

"I've been notified by a source in the Palm Beach Sheriff's Office that they have arrested the last of the gunmen who chased you and Andrés Carmen. Deputies from Broward have been called to come and question them tomorrow."

"That's a good thing, Billy," I said, reading the slight anxiety in his voice.

"True. But my information is that they belong to a well-documented gang up here, one that numbers some two dozen members."

"Right," I said. Sometimes Billy has the lawyer's way of circumlocution.

"The newest arrestee already admitted that there was some kind of Wild West–style bounty out on Andrés Carmen. I fear that just because they failed in their attempt doesn't mean the next level in their gang won't take the hit money offer."

"You need me to go up and get Andrés out of his girlfriend's trailer?"

"I would be remiss if I didn't at least try," he said.

"I'm on my way."

16

IT WAS LIKE being back walking a summer beat behind South Street in Philadelphia: middle of the night, sweat trickling down between my shoulder blades and settling in my waistband, eyes trying to adjust to the dark while searching every shadowed corner and parked vehicle with a clear shot at the trailer in which Andrés Carmen was still staying.

It was like sniffing out the drug runners and their hidey holes in the city. As a foot patrolman, I'd known most of the dealers who fed the appetites of the South Street crowd in the 1990s. It was always a game to actually catch them with product in their possession. Sometimes I'd win; sometimes not. But back when I was creeping the alleys, I had a badge and a gun. Tonight, even though I might find some gangbangers waiting to hit our friend Andrés, I was sneaking around with nothing but a PI business card in my pocket.

I'd parked the Gran Fury two blocks away and put on my old blue-black windbreaker just to give me some cover. The night was quiet and warm. And as I did a perimeter around the trailer, I tried not to underestimate the shooters who had fired first at me and Luz Carmen, and then had tried to chase down Andrés. Yes, you could write them off as idiot street criminals hard up for money now that the drug trade had moved to a more businesslike, hand-to-hand market. But these guys had been armed with automatic weapons. And they were brazen enough to stage a wild-ass car chase in the middle of the day. So would they not just storm Andrés's girlfriend's place if they knew he was there, and kill him the way same they tried to in the cul-de-sac?

Sure, that was an option. But I was hoping that wasn't going to happen while I was inside talking Andrés into leaving. Maybe my little surveillance here had more to do with self-preservation than trying to save the kid again.

As I tightened the circle around the trailer, I took in the sounds and smells of the beaten-down trailer park: the distinctive odor of overused kitty litter dumped behind one place; the leftovers from a recent fish-fry, stashed in an old-style metal garbage can, some procrastinating resident leaving it in the alley instead of at the pickup spot on the street. The overloud blabbing of a television sitcom spilled from a window screen along with canned laughter.

Closing in from the north, I spotted a misplaced light. Closer still, I finally made out some sort of battery-powered candle set on a picnic table. A young girl, middle-school age, was huddled over what looked like a fat textbook, with a pencil in hand, scratching at a notebook. From the trailer beside her came the noise of an argument between two adults. Something crashed inside, and the raw sound of flesh slapping flesh stung the air.

I watched the girl put her forehead down onto the open pages of the book. Though I tried to move away quietly, she looked up at the sound of my footfall, and we made eye contact. I raised my index finger to my lips. *Shssss.*

She rolled her eyes at me—whatever—and went back to her homework.

Finally, I stepped up to the door of Andrés's and looked first to the spot where Billy and I had seen the pit bull in the light of day. There appeared to be nothing there, though I was half-expecting a glowing pair of evil eyes. Taking one more glance behind me, I rapped on the door. It opened slowly, making that gum rubber sound of a seal being pried.

When I stepped into the light, I was greeted by the black-eyed barrel of an over-under shotgun. At the other end was the scrunched face of a blonde woman, her eyes narrowed to slits, her forehead furrowed beyond her age.

"Who the fuck are you?"

While my hands were shoulder-high, palms facing outward, I explained who I was, and that I did not deserve to die on the rusted iron steps of a faded Florida house trailer. The woman, small-boned and too defiant for her size, finally backed up, but did not put the shotgun down. When I stepped up into the entry, the smell of onion-fried liver hit my nose, which might have been pleasant under other circumstances, but in the claustrophobic space—already ripe with a scent of its own—I felt my stomach twinge.

The teenage kid was still on the couch as if he hadn't moved since the last time I was here. He cut his eyes to me for only long enough to assure his boredom, and then went back to the television screen running the same Grand Theft Auto game he'd been on before. He was about the same age as the girl out in the dark working on her studies. The juxtaposition made me feel sorry for him.

"Andrés," the woman screeched down the hall. "Your boy is here."

Your boy?

Andrés came out wearing a strap T-shirt that used to pass as white and the floppy blue scrub pants I presumed he wore at work.

"What's up?"

The girlfriend stepped back next to him as if to present some kind of united front. She was wearing a stained waitress uniform and looked ridiculous holding the big shotgun. I tried to relax my shoulders and clasped my hands in front of me, one holding the other like a salesman during a formal presentation.

I was controlling my anger.

"What's up? Is it that the Palm Beach Sheriff's Office found the guys who were trying to shoot you?" I said, watching the woman's dirty-green eyes to see if she'd been brought up-to-date on her boyfriend's escapades. She didn't flinch.

"And put that gun down before you accidentally hurt somebody," I added, now staring into the woman's eyes.

Andrés put his palm out and touched the gun barrel gently.

"It's OK, Cheryl," he said.

She looked disappointed, but sat down on a nearby rocking chair and laid the gun across her lap like a hillbilly—which she very well could have been, given her posture and ashen skin.

"Yeah, my friend told me he heard they popped the last guy over near the projects. So that's a good thing, right?" Andrés said. "They're just a bunch of gang assholes, anyway."

"Yeah, gang assholes," I said. "The operative word being gang, which means they're part of a bigger whole, along with others who share the same information, rumor, word on the street and all. You know—like the word that there's a price on your head.

"But since you've already been out there talking to your friends, you probably already know that, too, right? And since you've been out chatting, your friends also know where you are. They're probably out there yakking to others about that very fact."

Now I was pissed.

The girlfriend made a show of picking up a cigarette pack, tamping it down on the surface of the table next to her, and then opening it. Andrés looked as if he were waiting on her to respond to me. The woman picked a cigarette out of the pack and fit it between her lips.

"We ain't afraid of a bunch of gang punks," she said, her voice a pathetic, almost humorous tough-guy growl, the cigarette bouncing with her words.

I shook my head and looked at Andrés. "Like I offered earlier," I said. "I have a place you can go where they won't find you. You could stay there a few days until the cops get things cooled down a bit. Mr. Manchester is trying to get the feds to talk with your sister, and if they start taking her seriously, they could come in to give both of you witness protection."

Andrés looked away. The girlfriend rolled her eyes and lit the cigarette and whispered "Luz" with an edge of disgust.

I pulled a kitchen chair out from under the nearby table and put it in front of the woman. Then I sat down to indicate that I wasn't leaving until I got an answer. The place was silent but for the sound of the boy on the couch clacking buttons on his handheld controller.

When I followed his eyes to the television screen, I saw a caricature of a stubble-faced guy holding a handgun. The figure had obviously just crashed his car into a police cruiser. On the ground in front of him was a uniformed caricature of an officer. Stubble-face was shooting the cop as he lay on the street. Each time the boy punched his thumb on the controller, the gun would fire and the cartoon body of the cop would actually jerk. The kid kept doing it over and over again.

I could feel my lips tighten into a hard line. I flexed my fingers to loosen them. When the girlfriend tipped her head back to take another long drag off the cigarette, I snuck a look at her other hand to make sure her finger wasn't inside the trigger guard of the shotgun. It wasn't.

When she relaxed to savor the smoke in her lungs, I grabbed the barrel of the shotgun and ripped it from her in one quick motion. She started to yelp, but when I banged the end of the barrel down into the floor, she jumped, coughed out a belch of smoke, and remained silent.

Andrés wasn't moving. I looked over at the kid, his eyes gone big.

"Turn that thing off before I put this gun butt through the screen," I said, pointing the shotgun stock in the direction of both the television and the hallway. "Go crawl into the place where you sleep."

The kid looked at his mom, who turned away. Andrés stepped back to clear a path for the boy. The kid sneered at me, but turned off his game, got up, and left sullenly, taking his time—the only thing left to do to show his tail wasn't between his legs.

"Sit down," I said to Andrés, motioning him to the empty couch. With the butt of the gun as a visual aide, I directed the girlfriend, "Join him."

She copied the same slow motion as her son, but moved. I planted the muzzle of the gun onto the floor between my feet. When I felt I had Andrés's attention, I started.

"I talked with the guy you call the Brown Man today," I said. Andrés looked up at me without moving his chin. "He's a drug dealer who used to sell crack on the street to junk men and whores.

"He's probably doing the same thing now, but his clientele has changed and he's moved up off the corners and into your warehouse. Tell me what you know about him."

The girlfriend had stopped at the hallway corner and snuck a look at Andrés, who kept his head down, his eyes seemingly on the video game controller the boy had dropped on the floor.

"They said he's a bad dude and not to fuck with him," Andrés said. "Nobody but the guy who runs the place and the IT dude ever say anything to him. But he's OK to me. He says hello to me when he sees me."

"Like one of his punk runners," the girlfriend said with a little snort in her voice.

I was losing my patience. "Shut up or leave," I said, staring at her. She would not meet my eyes, but slouched against the wall.

I turned back to Andrés. "Is the Brown Man there all the time?"

"No. I only see him once in a while. But when he's there, everybody gets nervous, you know—uptight. Even the IT guy gets nervous, and all he does is the computer work. He don't have nothin' to do with the drugs."

"So the Brown Man's like the enforcer or something?"

"No. He ain't carryin' or nothin' like that. But they all straighten up when he's there, even the guy who's like the manager," Andrés said. "It's like he's got the juice, man, and everybody knows it."

It sounded like Carlyle had a trigger somewhere—the threat of exposure, of violence, of start-up money the operation was beholden to.

"Has he ever brought anyone else into the warehouse—someone like a partner?"

"Uh, uh, not like a partner. But he was with a dude once who I know was a Monroe Heights Posse."

"Gang member?"

"Yeah. They were looking at the product, you know, the drugs and shit."

"Same as the guys who were chasing you?"

"Nah, different crew, but from the same area in Riviera Beach, you know."

"No, I don't know," I said.

What I did know was that Carlyle, if he was even close to the businessman and investor he said he was, would have some pretty extensive contacts in the criminal world. And he wouldn't give up those contacts even as he supposedly rose beyond selling crack to prostitutes on the corner. If he'd somehow bled his old world into the new world of medical and prescription fraud, he wouldn't necessarily leave all his violent tactics of coercion and control behind, either.

I could go hash this all out with Billy, or I could sit here in a filthy trailer with a couple of brass-balled neophytes who weren't going to listen to an ex-cop anyway. I stood up and pushed the kitchen chair back behind me with my foot.

"I'm offering you a place to hide out one last time," I said. Neither of them moved.

I went to the door, turned the knob, and then let the shotgun fall to the floor. I'd had enough.

"Good luck then," I said, and left.

WHEN I GOT back to the Gran Fury, I climbed in and called Billy. Even though it was 1:00 A.M., he answered before the second ring.

"The kid won't move," I said. "His girlfriend has him under her thumb, and he isn't going to do anything that makes him look weak in her eyes."

"Machismo," Billy said.

"Comes with the territory."

Lots of people talk about personal responsibility. When idiots do stupid things that turn out badly, those same people still cry that someone else should have stepped in and saved them. There are times I get sick of it. Billy rarely does. He sees the good in people, despite the world that has unfolded in front of him since he was a skinny projects kid toughing it out in Northwest Philly.

"I say we turn him in, Max. We give the trailer location to the Palm Beach Sheriff's Office and let them arrest him on the outstanding warrant from the chase. At least in lockup he'll be safe," Billy said.

"Your call, Counselor," I said. "I'm going home."

17

AT 7:00 A.M., I was lying next to Sherry when my cell rang. It felt like I'd been in bed for ten minutes. The last vision in my head before falling asleep was of a young girl sitting in the dark, an opened textbook in front of her, her face illuminated by a white flame.

I reached out and flipped open the phone.

"I just got a call from my contact in the sheriff's office," Billy announced, his voice stoic and businesslike. "Andrés Carmen's trailer caught fire at four this morning. They found three bodies. I have to go tell Luz that her brother is dead."

"Jesus, Billy! When did you call in the loca—" But before I could finish, he hung up. I sat straight up, staring at the rippled light against the bedroom wall.

"What is it?" Sherry said. Her voice was sleepy, but as a cop she was always on alert for calls in the night.

"I've got to go," I said, swinging my feet out of the bed. "I think we lost some people we shouldn't have."

Sherry rolled up on one elbow.

"The Carmen family?"

The woman didn't miss much.

"The brother," I said, standing up and grabbing for my pants, which still seemed warm. "His girlfriend, and probably her teenage son."

Sherry was silent while I got dressed.

"You saved him once, Max," she said just before I left, a last-minute attempt to salve my soul.

* * *

I PARKED IN the same place I had just eight hours ago. When I opened the door to the Gran Fury, I could smell the place once again, this time differently. The odors of animal feces, cooked fish, and dry garbage were now overwhelmed by that of acidic smoke, melted plastic, and charred wood. My route was less circuitous this time. I didn't circle and watch. Instead, I walked straight to the spot where Andrés Carmen's trailer once stood, or as closely as the cops would allow.

A couple of community service aides were keeping onlookers at a fifty-foot distance, back behind the two fire engines that were still on the scene, spinning their red lights through the thick morning air. There was one sheriff's office patrol car parked where the driveway to the burned trailer used to be. The absence of a medical examiner's vehicle told me the bodies had already been removed. Residents stood in small clusters, some still dressed in housecoats or hurriedly tossed-on sweatshirts and sneakers. They watched the firefighters rooting through the ashes with crowbars and shovels, turning up clumps of curled aluminum and still smoking wood, as if some survivor were going to rise from the blackness to their astonishment and applause.

I noted a uniformed official standing at the center of the mass, about where I'd stood talking with Andrés and his girlfriend, Cheryl. The officer was videotaping the scene. The fire marshal, designated by his stenciled windbreaker, was at the north end, taking close-up photographs of something at his feet.

I stood and surveyed the area with my hands in my pockets. You didn't have to be an expert to see that there had been a sizable explosion. The burn pattern radiated out in streaks, and there was charring in the trees too high and away from where flames would have risen straight up from a normal fire. Soot flash covered the facing walls of both adjacent trailers, but there was no extensive fire damage. The picnic table where Billy, Andrés, and I sat two days earlier was flipped on its face, the wooden legs smoldering, but still intact. If I was guessing, ground zero would have been at the north end of the trailer where the bedrooms had been, and where the fire marshal was now. The trailer was obliterated there. What was left of the rest of the structure was peeled back like an enormous charred cigar that had been loaded with a stupid exploding tip.

Out of the corner of my eye, I caught a tiny knot of people off to the side. A tall, thin man dressed in black trousers and an oxford shirt and tie was bent over like a piece of angle iron, listening to a young girl. He turned his head and looked my way while the child averted her eyes and spoke quietly. I recognized her as the homework girl from my nighttime visit.

The angular man stood, nodded some sort of thank-you to the parents of the girl, and walked my way. As he approached, he took out a cell phone, made a quick call, and loosened his tie, like a guy who might have to run after something. I stood my ground even when, no, especially when, I saw the detective's shield clipped to his belt.

"Hey, how you doin'?" he said as he met my eyes. The accent made me think ex-New York cop, or inveterate watcher of bad television.

"All right. How *you* doin'?" I said, mocking the accent, even though I didn't have a reason to make my situation any worse. His eyes narrowed.

"I was ah, interviewing some neighbors. Witnesses," he said. "Do you live here?"

"No," I said, and then looked back at the burn. They hate it when you ignore them. I hated it when they ignored me. I wasn't sure why I was being a jerk.

"I'm Detective Sheldon Woller from the Palm Beach Sheriff's Office. I'd still like to speak to you."

Now the accent was gone. I looked back at him. He was younger than me by several years, had thinning brown hair, pale eyes, and dark frame glasses. He was almost my height, slim in the chest and right down through the hips—an athlete by the carriage, probably a long-distance runner or bicyclist. His shoulders weren't broad enough for a natural swimmer.

"I'll be glad to do so as soon as my lawyer gets here," I said, and continued watching the fire marshal as he bent to his knees and adjusted his camera.

Detective Woller took out a pad and pen, like a reporter.

"I'm going to need your name, sir."

"No, you won't," I said, continuing to look out at the marshal.

I heard the guy exhale in frustration. He stayed quiet for a few seconds, strategizing. Then, by the nature of his next question, he took a chance.

"My information is that you were in the area last night, sir," he finally said, mustering some authority to his voice. "Witnesses said you were sneaking through the neighborhood and that you were visiting the people who lived in this trailer shortly before the fire."

"Witnesses?" I said. "You mean a twelve-year-old who was doing her homework in the dark by candlelight while the boyfriend was beating the shit out of her mom inside?"

Given that I hadn't turned toward him, I couldn't see the open mouth of the detective, or the regathering of his face.

"Were you in that trailer last night, or weren't you?" Woller said, the tone of authority changing to pissed off. "In my experience, sir, arsonists like to come back and observe their handiwork. Maybe you'd like to take a trip with me to the station, and we can talk there?"

I had to admire the guy's persistence even in the light of the fact that I'd already mentioned my lawyer. He was questioning me without arrest or Miranda.

"In your experience? Does that mean you worked for ATF before you became a sheriff's detective?" I said. "Because it's ATF that investigates most incidences of arson down here. Or did you get that bit about the perp coming back to the scene of the crime from *CSI Miami*?"

This time, I turned and looked into Woller's face and saw his lips go into a solid line and his left hand reach behind his back, where I assumed his belt held his handcuffs. He kept the right hand free, hovering above the clip-on holster for his service weapon.

I couldn't blame him. I wouldn't put up with an asshole like me, either.

Fortuitously, and yes, coincidentally, I looked over the young detective's shoulder to see a familiar figure walking up the street. I held up my palm to Woller and said, "Look, I'm sorry, Detective, but before you arrest me, you'll have to deal with my lawyer, who's right behind you."

To his credit, Woller did not turn to look. He held my eyes until he heard Billy's voice.

"Detective Woller, I presume," Billy said in his pleasant greeting voice. "I come with t-tidings from your sergeant, Ray Lynch. M-May I and my investigator, Max Freeman, be of s-service to you, sir?"

Deferring to Billy, I took a step back. Woller put his hands back in front and clasped them, but watched me suspiciously.

"And how is it that you know Sergeant Lynch," the detective said to Billy. "Mister, uh . . ."

"Manchester," Billy said. "William Manchester." He offered his hand, and Woller shook it. "I've known Sergeant Lynch for s-several years and sp-spoke to him this morning on the way here.

"He informed m-me that you had b-been dispatched due to the deaths of three people. Apparently, it is st-standard to send a detective is such circumstances."

I watched Woller looking into Billy's face. If he was put off by the stutter, it didn't show. Whether he believed Billy had a connection with his boss, that didn't show, either. But I had to give him props for holding his tongue when most people would have started responding to Billy's statement.

"And . . . ?" he said simply.

"And we are here to offer any help we m-might," Billy said, gesturing to include me in the offer. "One of the victims was essentially a cl-client, a Mr. Andrés Carmen. Mr. Carmen was the apparent target of a recent gang sh-shooting, an attempt that was, in fact, thw-thwarted by Mr. Freeman."

Again, the detective did not immediately respond. I was only a little disappointed when he gave in.

"And you told Sergeant Lynch all of this?"

"Yes," Billy said.

"That's weird because it's always hard to get Rich in the morning. He's usually taking his kids to school," the detective said.

"I don't know about Rich, but Sergeant Lynch's first name is Ray, and his t-twin girls are in college up in Gainesville," Billy said, maintaining his stoic face, even though the detective had essentially just called him a liar. "If you are skeptical, Detective, you should call the sergeant and verify who I am rather than try to game me," Billy said, and offered Woller his cell phone. "His p-private number is at the top of the recently dialed list."

Woller kept his hands clasped. I figured he was probably new to the squad, unsure about bothering his boss. He wanted to show he could handle such simplicities on his own.

"OK, Mr. Manchester," he said. "We removed the bodies early at sunup. The ME here is very good, and with all due respect to the dead, we didn't want to have to take them out with the news helicopters and shit birds clustering around."

Shit birds—I'd heard the term before. Cops used it to refer to the rubberneckers and ambulance sniffers who always show up when there's ghoulishness in the air.

The detective nodded toward the pile of ash. "The marshal determined they were all in their beds in the back when the gas exploded."

"Gas?" Billy said.

"It's an old-style trailer, with a propane gas tank and line to the interior heater. The marshal is going on the theory that the connection rusted out or separated with age and filled the back end of the trailer with gas," Woller said. "Someone inside lit a cigarette, and boom!"

I thought of the girlfriend, recalled the bobbling Marlboro on her lip.

"The ME didn't find anything obvious before they carted them off to the morgue, but then they were burned pretty badly," Woller continued.

"If they don't find any sign of these people being tied up or shot or bludgeoned or of the gas line being tampered with, they'll end up calling it accidental."

"Even if there was a recent attempt on Andrés Carmen's life?" I said, jumping in for the first time.

"Forensics, Mr. Freeman," Woller said, now looking at me. "Unless you get someone to talk, it'll sit for months on the crime scene backlog. Unless someone high up the line takes an interest. Shit, you know—you were a cop."

I matched his look, searching his face, maybe letting the surprise show on my own features. "That obvious?"

"Pretty much," the detective said. "You're working as a PI—probably retired from up north somewhere. Hard to cover up the look of a man out of uniform."

"So you've already ditched the lead that the little girl gave you?"

"What little girl would that be?"

"The one who said she saw me poking around last night."

He shook his head, looked away, and smiled a little.

"Can't blame me, man. You gotta take what you can get."

"I'd have done the same," I said, and finally offered my hand. As he shook it, I looked over his shoulder and watched Billy walk gingerly toward the fire marshal. I tried to hold the detective's focus for another few seconds to give Billy the chance to ask his questions.

"Anybody see any other suspicious strangers in the night?" I asked. "Maybe a couple of gangbangers tossing flaming bottles through a window?"

"No. And nobody heard anything, either, until they were nearly blown out of their own beds at four in the morning."

"Lucky," I said, taking another peek at Billy.

But the detective picked up on it and turned. "Hey," he yelped. "Hey, Manchester, you can't go in there." As he started toward Billy and the marshal, the detective turned and gave me an appropriately dirty look.

Twenty minutes later, Billy and I were standing at his Lexus out beyond the entrance to the trailer park. Billy had gotten little from the fire marshal. Woller was pissed enough to tell us both that if we wanted any more information, it would have to come through "your friend Sergeant Lynch," and that we would be banned from the fire scene unless we were in the sergeant's presence.

"Was it worth losing a good source in the sheriff's office," I said to Billy, who was scrolling through a contact list on his cell phone.

"It won't be a loss," he said without looking up from the screen. He punched in a number and looked out at the tree line. After a couple of seconds, he said, "Yes, I'll wait."

"The marshal was more helpful than he w-wanted to b-be," Billy said, twisting the microphone end of the phone away from his mouth while keeping the earpiece near.

"He was still tracing the gas p-piping to the outside tank but hadn't reached an end point. He's going to have to f-find the outside f-fixture and then determine if it was tampered with. He said it's p-possible it could have rusted loose or simply fallen apart. The salt in the ocean air down here p-plays havoc on anything whether it's copper or aluminum or even wood."

"So at least they're looking at the possibility that someone blew up the place," I said.

"Yes. Jim Fisher, please," Billy said into the phone. Then to me, "I'm not s-sure how hard they'll look. But yes, they are entertaining the p-possibility."

"So what did he tell you that he didn't want to tell you?" I asked.

But Billy was back on the phone. Usually, I find this kind of cell phone etiquette rude, but Billy can get focused. And after all, he's my friend, not some dork talking to his girlfriend while having a conversation with me.

"Yes, Jim. Fine, how are you? Yes, well, I've got a bit of a job for you. Right up your alley, my friend. There was a trailer home fire out in Lantana, and the remains of a dog have been left at the scene.

"No, actually, the known family are all dead. The authorities have no interest in dead dogs, but I do.

"Yes, you will have permission to remove the remains. Are you able to do that?

"No. I need the results of the necropsy as soon as possible. Yes. Yes. I'm sending you a text with the address right now. Thank you, Jimmy."

Billy folded the phone and looked out at the tree line, thinking.

"The dog?" I said.

"Did you m-miss that gang of flies buzzing the corner of the fence line? That's unlike you," Billy said.

I shrugged, and looked stupidly back toward the fire scene, even though it was impossible to see it from here.

"Can you imagine that p-pit bull letting someone crawl in and uncouple a gas line and set a fuse or light a candle or whatever under that trailer w-without taking a bite out of said someone?"

"No," I said, remembering the eyes of the beast. "No, I can't."

18

I DON'T DO sympathy well. I know this.

As a cop, I was useless at consolation when family would arrive at a shooting scene. I could not watch relatives wail at fatal accident scenes. "I'm sorry for your loss" seems rudely inadequate in the face of death.

I know I made improvements in this lack of empathy after Sherry's surgery when I spent hours at her bedside, mostly just watching her sleep, watching helplessly as every twitch and mild groan worked at my insides. I was at fault for her pain, and helpless.

I was sure she saw through my reassuring smiles when she awakened. My inane, happy talk ramblings sounded insincere even to my own ears. My kisses hello and good-bye seemed dry and perfunctory. One day when her strength was up, Sherry finally told me to get lost. She said she'd call me when they released her to go home. But I was in the bedside chair the next morning when she awoke.

"I am sorry for your loss," I said to Luz Carmen as I stood uncomfortably before her in the living room of Billy's seaside hideaway in Deerfield Beach. She did not look up. One of her woman friends, whom Billy had brought to comfort her, had an arm around Carmen's shoulders, and looked up into my eyes as she subtly shook her head.

I went back outside and stared at the breaking waves on the ocean, silently thanking this woman for my dismissal.

At the fire scene, Billy said he would wait for his man to come and collect the remains of the pit bull. He also wanted to get on his cell to badger the federal authorities to take steps to protect Luz Carmen as a criminal enterprise whistle-blower.

In the meantime, he dispatched me to his seaside getaway to watch over her. Early this morning, Billy had convinced Luz Carmen to avoid the fire scene until authorities determined when she could see her brother's body. After witnessing the molten ash of the trailer, I doubted that event was ever going to take place. There would not be much left of Andrés Carmen, and certainly there could be no comfort in viewing his charred remains.

For the entire drive from the fire, I'd been rolling the facts of what we knew around in my head, grinding away at what didn't fit, the coincidences that left gouges in any known pattern. I sat down on a retaining wall just outside the villa, put my feet on the beach sand, and watched nature do the same thing, the in and out of the tide smoothing each piece of shell, coral, and stone down to a grain.

Like a good investigator, Billy had put himself inside the head of the killer, if there indeed was a killer. While I was foolishly tossing around thoughts of how a group of gangbangers would throw a Molotov cocktail into the trailer, he was thinking how a quiet assassin would sneak onto the lot, crack the gas line, and then set some sort of fuse that would grant him clear distance before the place exploded. In that scenario, the guy would have had to get past the dog. How did he silence the beast?

While I chastised myself, I sensed movement behind me and turned to see Luz Carmen's friend slip out the door of the villa. She approached me across the patio. *"Perdóname,"* she said, then caught herself and reworked her statement in broken English.

"Ms. Luz should try to eat, sir. It is no good to lose strength."

"Yes, of course," I said. The friend was older than Carmen and had a more distinctly Latin look. She was small, her hair was shot with gray, and her hands were those of a workwoman, coarse and wrinkled.

"There is a restaurant called the Bru's Room down the way," I said, fishing my car keys and some twenties out of my wallet. "Ask for Patti and tell her it is for Mr. Freeman. She knows me. Get whatever you think is best."

The woman took the money, looking hesitant, but repeating the name of both the restaurant and Patti.

"I would go myself," I said, feeling a need to explain. "But I can't leave Ms. Carmen again."

The woman nodded and moved off, again repeating the restaurant name and that of the bartender I knew there. After she'd gone, I pulled a patio chair closer to the door of the bungalow. Within a few minutes, Billy called me on the cell phone.

"Are you with Luz Carmen?" he said without any preamble, unusual for the almost painfully well-mannered Billy.

"Yeah, she's right here. Her friend went for lunch," I said, matching his curtness. "What'd you find out?"

"The dog was shot, Max, once in the head with a 147-grain round. My man who did the necropsy says the shooter put the muzzle of the gun right up to the animal's head and fired."

The cop at the fire scene hadn't said anything about neighbors hearing a gunshot in the night, or anything other than the explosion that rocked them out of their beds.

"Silencer?" I said, thinking out loud.

"No way to know for sure," Billy said. "He's a veterinarian, not a ballistics guy. It was lucky he had a scale to weigh the slug."

"It still ought to put the accidental fire theory on the shelf," I said.

"Someone came after Andrés and tried to make it look like an accident. Whoever it was didn't know about the dog. It surprised him at some point, and he had to kill it so he could set the fire."

"However it happened, it makes me even more concerned for Luz's safety," Billy said, showing a bit more emotion now. "The fed's bureaucratic response is going to be slow, Max."

"I'll take her out to the shack. We should have done that to begin with," I said, thinking of the brother. The only saving grace was that it a gas flash fire. They may have died quickly, maybe without ever awakening from their sleep. It was something, but not much.

"It's not going to be a request this time," I said. "I'm heading for the Glades now, Billy."

"Let me know when you get settled. I'm taking the Carmen's cause to a higher authority," Billy said. "Maybe I can get some judicial pressure going."

"Good luck," I said, and punched off the cell.

I knocked lightly at the door of the bungalow and opened the door. Luz Carmen was on the couch, curled up like a child, her face in a pillow, her knees folded up, her feet tucked under her.

"Ms. Carmen, when your friend gets back, we're going to have to move again," I said, trying to keep my tone even, no urgency, but still strong enough for her to know there was no choice. "We're going to a place where you'll be safe. I'll take you by your home to collect some things."

The woman did not move and it scared me at first. I took a step closer.

"Ms. Carmen. Did you hear me?"

This time, I could see her dark head move slightly, nodding in assent.

"You'll be OK," I said. "Mr. Manchester will make sure you'll be safe."

"It does not matter," she said, her voice muffled and scratchy from pain and from crying, but level in its acceptance. "I have killed my own brother."

I took two more steps across the small tiled floor and sat only on the edge of the couch. I had no intention of touching her or trying to console. Hell, I wasn't even sure of my motivation. She had to know I was there, but did not move.

"Every one of us is responsible for our own actions," I said out into the empty room. I didn't tack her name onto the end of the statement. Maybe I wasn't speaking only to her; maybe she wasn't the only one who needed to hear the words out loud. "Your brother made his choices; you couldn't be his keeper forever."

Piety usually brings silence, and this was no exception. The room was still quiet when the door opened and Carmen's friend came in holding a large plastic bag. Her eyes went from me to Carmen, a quick assessment, and then back.

"Is she good?"

I only nodded and stood.

"Try to get her to eat, and then we'll have to go."

The woman looked confused.

"It's not safe here. I'm taking her somewhere else. She and I will go in my car. You stay here for a few minutes after we leave, and then go home," I said. "Did you notice anyone outside, anyone who looked suspicious? Someone watching you? Someone by my car?"

The woman shook her head.

"No," she said.

"Are you sure?"

"A black man, walking," she said. "He was alone. Another man, old, with a dog."

I could tell I was scaring her into seeing danger in everyone.

"It's OK. Eat," I said, standing and crossing to the door. "I'll be right out here."

I figured I'd give them half an hour. It was already 1:00 P.M., and if we were going to get to Luz Carmen's house so she could pack a few things, and then get out to the boat ramp at the park on my river, we'd be losing light fast. I didn't mind canoeing out to the shack in the dark, but I didn't want to freak out Carmen. The darkness and secluded wildness of the place can do that to the most adventurous soul, and I didn't think the woman's head was anywhere near that state.

Maybe she was still in shock over the loss of her brother. Maybe she was internalizing her remorse over bringing him into her decision to blow the whistle on the Medicare scam. But if I could quietly reassure her that I could keep her safe until the ring was broken, or until the feds took over by giving her protection, I'd be ahead of the game.

To that end, I decided not to tell her about Billy's and my theory that the person who killed her brother was not part of the gangbanger crew who fired at us to scare her off, or the ones who tried to kill

Andrés on the road. We weren't giving up on a connection; there were too many coincidences. But a guy who does a drive-by or a high-speed chase doesn't go to the trouble of using a silenced kill shot on a dog, and then jury-rig a gas explosion to look like an accident. We were dealing with two completely different styles. I was more wary of the sneaky one, the planner. It was always harder to see his kind coming.

As I walked down the slate stone path to check out the parking lot hard on A1A, I kept the front of the bungalow in sight. On the street, a middle-aged woman jogged by. A tight group of bicyclists, all dressed in the same colors, went whizzing by. A family with a mom wearing a big straw hat and the kids wielding sand pails, were unloading from the van next to my Gran Fury. The father was lugging the beach chairs and the coolers—way too domestically harassed to be an assassin.

When I went back to the bungalow, the door came open a crack as I walked up.

"OK, she is ready," Carmen's friend said.

"Did she eat?"

"A little. I put the rest in the bag for you."

Luz was standing with her head down, as if she were only moving at the direction of her friend, with no motivation or decision-making power of her own. Draped over her head was a shawl I had not seen before, which gave her the appearance of a villager or bag lady, the opposite of the confident, order-giving semi-professional I'd met a few days ago.

"OK," I said, handing the friend another couple of twenties. "Wait at least fifteen minutes after we go, and then take a cab home. I don't want you to be seen with us. You're out of it, ma'am. Thank you for helping."

The woman still seemed a bit mystified as I took Luz by the elbow and led her down the path. It would have been a long shot for someone to find this place. But even if someone was watching us, looking for an opportunity, I hoped their focus would be on my car, not on the bungalow.

At the Gran Fury, I guided Luz into the passenger seat and put the package of food in the back, the odor of black beans and rice and homemade meat loaf rising out of the bag. Patti had done them right, giving the woman the best comfort food in the place. I was starving, but I could wait.

I checked again for anyone unusual in the area, and then backed out into traffic and checked the rearview. I was confident I could pick up a trail if there was one. But just in case, while I had the opportunity, I timed the lights and burned the green ones deep yellow before punching it through the intersection. I got a few appropriate horns, but no one followed us. I had to believe that the shack would be the safest place on Earth.

19

AT HER HOUSE, it took Luz Carmen twenty minutes to pack. As dazed as she was, she probably would have taken more if she'd been her typical, businesslike, responsible self. But where we were going did not require the right clothes, the right toiletries, or any makeup whatsoever. I told her to bring three days' worth and to put everything in one fabric bag, waterproof if possible.

When I said it, she didn't even look twice at me. A woman in any other circumstance would have called the cops. She hadn't said a word during the drive, her eyes hooded and looking out the passenger-side window; what she was actually seeing was not mine to know.

While she packed, I searched the inside of the townhouse. When we'd first arrived, I made her stay in the car while I scoured the outside, inspecting the door locks both front and back, the windows to make sure they were secure, and the fuse box and power cables to make sure they hadn't been tampered with. Still I made her give me the key and I entered first, searched each room, and checked the stove, which fortunately was electric. Only then, did I allow her to come into her own home.

While Luz was packing, I called Sherry on my cell.

"It was them, right?" she said when she picked up.

"Yeah, like I figured—the son, his girlfriend, and her boy."

Sherry let the silence fill the earpiece for a few seconds. She was a career cop, too; three dead, she'd been there before.

"What about the sister? Is she with anyone?"

"Me," I said. "I'm taking her to the shack where she'll be safe."

Until the words were out of my mouth, I didn't think about how that would sound to Sherry. The last time she'd been to the shack, she'd ended up losing her leg.

I told her about the fire, how the investigators were leaning toward an accidental gas explosion; but that Billy had called in one of his connections, who discovered that the family pit bull had been killed with a shot to the head before the fire.

"So is Palm Beach putting their homicide people on it?" she said.

"They probably are now. And we may all be getting a bit paranoid, but Billy didn't think his place in Deerfield was safe enough for Luz. I'm taking her to the shack until he can convince the feds to get a whistle-blower protection clearance for her."

"So you're going to stay there until that's done," Sherry said.

"Yeah, I'll stop on the way to the river and get enough supplies for a couple of days and see how it goes. The woman's pretty messed up, but she's not freaking out or anything."

"Does she have family? Do they know what's happened?"

"Her friend said she and the brother left all their family in Bolivia and Carmen rarely talked about them. She's got a cell phone with her. I'm trying not to push her," I said, realizing that Sherry was thinking all of the personal things you do after a death in the family that I'd just glossed over in a rush to keep the woman safe.

"She's going to need help, Max. Counseling help," Sherry said. "You know that, right?"

There it was again, the stubborn one who couldn't see herself in the mirror.

"Yeah, I know. If the feds get her into a safe house someplace, maybe they can set that up, but right now I . . ." Right now I didn't know what the hell to do other than what we were doing.

"Well, that might not be long," Sherry said. The lead-in was obvious in the tone of her voice.

"Why? What's happening?" I said.

"The sheriff wasn't as slow on the uptake as we figured he'd be on that warehouse, Max," she said. "They put a team together and raided the place this morning, thinking they'd find the computer boys hard at work."

"And?"

"The bad guys were ahead of us. When the team blew into the place, it had already been cleared out. There was a loading dock out the backside, and they must have trucked everything away in the middle of the night. There were a few computer cables, some empty boxes of printout paper, some generic office supplies, and a few empty desks."

"Shit," I said.

"But there was enough left behind to convince our guys to start a bigger pursuit. There's plenty on the record of other operations in Dade and Palm Beach Counties, so they're going to compare notes and do some interagency sharing. If they get a task force together, you know they're going to want to talk to your friend Ms. Carmen."

Good news—very good news. But I could tell from Sherry's voice that there was more. Sometimes when she's in an investigative mode, she holds back when she's sharing her work with me, like a storyteller who is saving the punch line.

"What else?" I said, doing my part as audience.

"Well, maybe the guys clearing out the warehouse were only interested in the medical fraud and didn't give a shit about the drugs, but they were sloppy," Sherry said. "No one left drugs, but they did leave behind the boxes that Andrés described to you."

We'd done this a lot in the old days, before the accident, try to outguess each other on investigations others were running—speculating on what they would find, or how they should have worked their cases. It was classic one-upmanship. It was a bit of a game for us, one I realized I'd been missing for the last several months.

"Ahhh, OK," I said, thinking. "Packaging, right?"

"Serial numbers, you big dope," she said. "Lot numbers for the drugs. The task force might be able to use them to track where the drugs came from: the hospitals, pharmacies, doctors' offices that originally purchased them."

"And any idiot users who still have the original containers," I said, trying to save face.

"Right," Sherry said with a little triumphant lilt in her voice. "Your client's brother, Andrés, is speaking to us from the grave, Max. Maybe that will be some comfort to his sister down the line."

"You could be right," I said. "I'll keep you updated, babe. I love you. Bye."

I will be the first one to admit that terms of endearment don't come naturally to me. For a moment, I wondered if this was something I'd been trying to teach myself since Sherry lost her leg, an almost unconscious realization that I could have lost her completely. After I slipped the cell phone back in my pocket, I saw that Luz was standing at the top of the stairs with a large ripstop nylon bag at her feet.

"I'm ready," she said.

It's an hour's drive up I-95 and then west to the state park where I kept my canoe at a boat ramp on the river. Along the way, we stopped to pick up supplies at a Winn-Dixie. Luz went inside with me, now unwilling to be anywhere but at my side. Now that she'd had some time to put things in perspective, she was scared. By the time we arrived at the boat ramp, it was late afternoon.

When I pulled up into a spot near the park ranger's Old Florida–style cabin, Dan Griggs came out to greet me. He was in a pair of khakis and had an old flannel shirt over his uniform. Ninety degrees and the old-timer looked like he was chilled. Or maybe he just didn't like the show of epaulets and insignias. He wore a pair of old black galoshes on his feet, the kind with the thin metal clips, but they were splayed open and flapped when he walked.

"Hey, Mr. Freeman, how you doin'?"

"Dan."

"I was startin' to think maybe I ought to put a FOR SALE sign on your canoe there," he said, subtle humor in his voice.

I smiled at the trust it showed. Old Florida country folks do not grant that trust easily to outsiders, and it had taken me some time to earn it from Dan. A few years ago when I was new to the river, I'd brought a tragedy with me. The longtime and locally beloved ranger had been killed by a criminal drawn to this place in part by me. I wasn't complicit in his death, but I wasn't blameless, either. And even though I would eventually get retribution for the loss of their friend, the locals did not forget easily.

"I hope you would have split the asking price with me, Dan," I said while I unloaded. We shared the joke with complimentary smiles.

Dan was doing one of those "looky here" strolls around the polished Gran Fury and was about to utter some *whooo-eee* utterances when Luz Carmen stepped out of the passenger-side door. The ranger quickly took his hat off and said, "Ma'am."

I introduced the two and told Dan that Ms. Carmen would be staying out in the shack for a few days "for some peace and quiet." He nodded and grabbed one of the grocery bags and followed me to the stand of palmetto trees where I stored my canoe.

"Well, you'll surely get that, ma'am. We do have quiet in abundance out here."

I winced at the language. It always amazed me how so-called country folk can find sophisticated articulation when they want to. Dan's predecessor, the Old Florida cracker who'd been killed, used this homey technique to his advantage, acting unworldly as a cover while he intensely studied and read everyone he met. I doubted that Dan's intention was the same, but he'd learned from a master. He knew Sherry, knew we were a couple; the presence of an attractive Latin woman suddenly on the scene would have intrigued him.

Luz did not respond to his comment, and only stepped closer to me.

Dan helped me flip my canoe, and while I wiped away some accumulated webs and their weavers—a couple of golden silk spiders that scrambled away into the brush—he went to fetch my paddles, which they kept in the ranger station when I was away. I dragged the sixteen-foot canoe down to the edge of the river and then started packing in the fresh water, canned goods, a couple of bags of ice, and some fresh vegetables and odd perishables from the grocery. Included was a twelve-pack of Rolling Rock in bottles that I never traveled to the shack without.

Dan returned with my wood-carved paddles and the chemical toilet I ferried to and from the shack, as well. It was originally designed for a sailboat, and worked fine in the backcountry. Because of the pristine nature of this river and its designation as a National Wild and Scenic River, restrictions on pollutants were tight. My adherence to the rules was one of the things that kept the state from tossing me out of the shack, which Billy owned, and which had been grandfathered in when they'd turned the area into a state park.

While I'd been packing, Luz had twisted her long dark hair into a rope and secured it with some band from her pocket.

"Have you ever been in a canoe?" I asked, and she held out her hand, motioning me to give her one of the paddles.

"I have been many times in a dugout on the rivers of my native Bolivia, Mr. Freeman," she said. "I will be fine."

I simply nodded and watched her carefully step into the bow and sit. Before shoving off, I turned to Dan. "Your buddy Joey will be dropping off my truck when he's finished fixing her," I said. "Give me a call, eh? We should be out here a couple of days."

"Will do, Mr. Freeman," he said. "Enjoy."

ALTHOUGH I ALWAYS felt a certain internal cleansing every time I came out to the shack, the memories of last year's damaging trip had not stopped diminishing that feeling. That disastrous outing would stick in my head forever. And as long as Sherry had to live with the loss of her leg, I would have to live with my bad planning and poor choices and foolish perception that modern man is somehow immune from the whims of nature and the whims of the human animal that resides in all of us.

Still, there was something about the movement of a craft over water, the undulation of liquid over a thin skin of a boat hull, and the leaving of noise and machinery and stop signs and unnatural lighting that calms even the most turbulent soul.

My river flows from gathered water in an Everglades basin that is well inland, and then follows a twisting path east to the ocean. Because of the ocean tides, the water into which we pushed can be silently swift, or eerily still. Because I was familiar with her watermarks on the shoreline, I guessed we were near slack tide, and wasn't disappointed when we glided out onto a surface that was flat and seemingly unshifting.

As I settled into the stern seat, I watched Luz Carmen's back and her handling of the paddle. She was perfectly balanced, careful yet strong with her stroke. After a few minutes, she was leaving a nice swirl in the water when she feathered the stroke, and then reached out for the next. I was not only satisfied that she wasn't going to accidentally flip us; it looked like we might make good time.

Once we caught a good rhythm, the boat moved smoothly and easily. Because of the load we were carrying, there was little glide, but the prow still cut nicely through the water and left a defined V behind us. I said little except to call out a direction, or to indicate the next curve of land to aim for. Luz only nodded and kept her thoughts to herself. Within an hour, the shoreline had morphed from sandy pines to low grasses spiked with the occasional tall bald cypress.

Because of the saltwater intrusion caused by man-made canals and the simple thirst of South Florida's population draining the freshwater aquifer below us, even this protected area showed the signs of nature under siege. The indigenous grasses were being invaded by cattails. The sable palms were losing their foliage, and their trunks were rotting from the creeping salt. Still, being out here was like a massage to the back of my neck, the thumbs of nature rubbing my temples. I realized I was breathing deeply again and was surprised at the way I had somehow forgotten how to do that while living in the city. By the time the banks narrowed and we reached the entry into the deep canopy of trees of the upper river, I was ready to let the shadowed greenness of my home fold over me.

In minutes, we were in a different world. The light changed: The overhead covering of leaves and cypress boughs created a kind of green cheesecloth, filtering the sun and creating streaks of sunlight that dappled the ferns and pond apple leaves lining the banks. The tea-colored water absorbed the sun, at points glowing as it reflected off spots where the bottom was pure white sand. The temperature fell several degrees, the shade diminishing the heat of the sun and cooling the air enough that it chilled our sweaty skin.

And the quiet we'd been enjoying was dampened even more by the closeness of thick foliage. A thousand years slipped away—ten thousand.

While we moved up stream, Luz Carmen sat mesmerized, her paddle resting across her knees, her head turning from side to side. A turtle the size of a dinner plate slipped off a downed tree trunk and disappeared into the water. Twenty yards away, a great blue heron stood on a spur of sand, its snakelike neck and sharp beak pointing out like an Egyptian hieroglyphic dancer. It gave us a few more yards and then spread its five-foot wingspan like a cape and flapped up into the air, disappearing upriver with a harsh squawk.

Luz couldn't help herself and turned to see if I had been a witness; I allowed a small smile. She did not, though her eyes were still big from the sighting.

"My place is about a half-mile more," I said. "Watch for the cypress knees. The water is kind of low."

Luz only nodded her head and put her paddle back in the water, stroking slowly. Farther up, we slid toward a gathering of knees, a protruding part of the cypress's root system that can gouge the hull of a canoe, but Luz used an impressive J-stroke to avoid them. The maneuver relaxed me. I made a note to ask where she'd learned it. Out here, there would be time to talk. I was confident she couldn't keep up her silence forever.

By the time we reached the entrance to my place, the afternoon light was fading fast. As we approached two towering bald cypress trees that some believed where at least four hundred years old, I directed Luz to steer in between them. Through this entrance, we slipped onto a short channel of still water that led us through some giant ferns and leather-wood shrubs until the water opened up to reveal my shack.

Built in the early 1900s, the structure is a small, eighteen-foot cube with a spiked roof that sits up in the air on four sturdy pilings. The water surrounds but never touches the "house." We maneuvered up to the small dock and once I had a strong hand on the deck, Luz expertly balanced herself on one foot on the centerline of the hull, rose, and stepped out. I lashed the boat to the dock. Then without a word of instruction, Luz began accepting the supplies as I handed them up out of the boat.

When we were set, I looked carefully at the weatherworn steps of my staircase. Out here in the swamplike humidity, anyone using the steps would leave a visible footprint behind, like a sunrise golfer on a dewy morning. Yes, the rain might wash away the markings, but I still used the early warning system as a way to tell if I'd had visitors. Today it looked clean, so I picked up some of the bags and headed up. At the top, while I keyed the padlock on the front door, I pointed out the oak barrel and nozzle that I used for a shower.

"A rain barrel shower is something you'll never forget if you're a city kid," I said to Luz, who had gathered her own bag and followed me up.

"I remember," she said, looking up at the contraption, which was little more than a short length of hose leading from a gasketed hole in the bottom of the barrel. Only one of the four roof gutters fed water into the open top, but it was always enough.

It's a crude device, and rare. But when I looked at Luz Carmen to explain her comment about recollecting such a thing, she turned without offering more. I didn't probe. I reminded myself that I knew very little of this woman and her life, both past and present. If she was going to open up, she'd do it on her time.

When I pushed the door open and stepped into my shack, I was met by the odor of must and mildew, inescapable in this environment. I dropped the bags and immediately went to the windows, opening the sashes one at a time for air flow and pushing open the Bahama shutters to let in the remaining light outside. Then I lit the kerosene lantern and placed it in the middle of the big, door-size table that dominated the middle of the room. The light spread a coppery glow throughout the place.

Luz was still standing just inside the door, her bag in her hand.

I nodded toward the bunk beds against the opposite wall.

"If you don't mind, I like the lower one," I said. When Sherry had come out, we put both mattresses together on the floor and dealt with the gap in the middle. That was obviously not in the plan this time.

Saying nothing, Luz deftly swung her bag in an arc up onto the top bunk. Again, I was surprised by her athleticism. Then she did a sweep of the place: the two mismatched pine armoires where my clothing and books were stored; the row of cupboards; the butcher block countertop; a pre-electric ice box at one end, and slop sink at the other; and the walled-off corner where the chemical toilet would be kept. I didn't have to explain that it wasn't much.

"It was originally built by a visiting industrialist from the northeast who used it for hunting and fishing trips," I said, feeling a need to say something in the cabin's defense. "Then in the 1950s, it was used by scientists who were studying the Everglades, mapping the moving water and doing marine population surveys."

Luz nodded her head as if it made perfect sense.

"Billy either bought it or accepted it in payment from some client. I rent it from him."

Again, she barely acknowledged me. I was starting to feel like a babbling idiot. I went back out and brought up the rest of the supplies.

When everything was put away, I rekindled the fire in the potbellied stove, scooped out coffee from a three-pound can into my old metal pot, and waited for the boil. Luz had taken a seat in one of two straight-backed chairs that flanked the table and was seemingly watching the flame of the kerosene lantern that I'd set in front of her. The shadows played on her face, creating an even deeper sense of sadness, if that were possible after losing a brother and blaming yourself for his death.

I sat down on the opposite side of the table and determined that I would not say "so how are you holding up" or some other inane comment.

Outside the night buzz had begun, with myriad insects, lizards, and bats doing the whole nocturnal dance of "eat and be eaten." When I first moved out here from Philadelphia, I thought the sounds would drive me crazy. My urban ear was in tune, or able to tune out, the constant sound of cars and horns, yelps and sirens, late-night television through an open window and predawn garbage trucks in nearby alleys. I thought I could sleep through anything. But the sound of nature in its nighttime chaos was so unsettling it took me months to rejigger my brain.

"You get used to it," I said, making a passing comment on what I was listening to without thought of what Luz was tragically carrying in her own head. She cut her eyes up into mine. And if she'd said "fuck you" to my face, she would have been justified. "The night sounds, I mean," I said quickly, trying to cover.

Her face relaxed, but only a bit.

"I have heard it before, when I was a girl. We would visit with my aunt in Rurrenabaque, where the jungles are thick and the animal life is abundant."

"In Bolivia?"

"Yes. My parents lived just outside La Paz. But my mother's people came from the area to the north on the Río Beni, which is very junglelike."

"And that's where you learned to use a canoe paddle?" I said, grateful that she was even speaking.

"Yes, in dugouts. My many cousins taught me. It was the way they traveled to most places. And they fished at night, spearing the *ranas,* uh, frogs."

"Ahh, frogs' legs," I said with an honest appreciation of the delicacy I had out in the Glades with my old friend Nate Brown after a night of spotting them with bright lights, and then spearing them with barbed spears. Maybe Luz saw my own slight smile; a pleasant twitch played at the corner of her mouth, remembering.

"Yes. We would cook them over the open fire in the night with the sparks flying up into the stars." She was staring into the flame now, seeing her past.

"And gator tail?" I said, trying to string some conversation together.

"No. No alligator," she said. "I saw your alligator on the way in, a small one, up on the bank."

She had a sharp eye. I had missed seeing any of the many gators that live along the river.

"We have caimans in Rurrenabaque—dark and nasty. We were always afraid of them as children. They were much too ugly and dangerous, or so we thought. But we have freshwater dolphins there. When they are young, they have very pink skin—very pretty, prettier than your gray ones."

She was reaching for more pleasant memories, a good sign, I thought.

"Did you and your brother see them together? The pink dolphins, I mean?"

"A few times, when he was young; then our parents moved closer to the city and worked all the time. But the neighborhoods in La Paz are not that different from parts of Miami. I went to school and Andrés went to the streets, to his friends and their street ways. It was after I came here and had a job that I brought him to live in America."

To save him, I thought, but didn't go there.

"So is your family still in Bolivia?" I said instead, thinking family connection in a time of grief.

"Some distant relatives—but our parents are gone."

Nice try, Max. I pushed away from the table and went to my so-called kitchen.

"Are you hungry? I can heat something up. Soup, maybe?"

"No thank you," Luz said.

I busied myself, finding a saucepan and going through my cupboard. It may be ironic in this place of water and so close to the sea, but my favorite soup is still the canned Bookbinder's lobster bisque from Philadelphia, which I buy a case at a time in a market in Fort Lauderdale and leave here. Billy would disown me if I asked for it at his place. Sherry only wrinkles her nose at any mention of the stuff; when I'm here, I indulge. You have to thicken the bisque by adding milk, so I always like to eat it the first day I come out, when I've just brought fresh milk for the cooler.

I pushed a few more pieces of dry pine into the stove to get the heat up and then opened the can, mixed it in the pan, and set it to simmer. Fortunately, the shack is built in the style of Old Florida dwellings. The inside ceiling is no ceiling at all. The roof slants up in four planes like a pyramid, the triangles coming together twenty feet above and meeting at a cupola that's vented at the top. The heat inside the cabin rises to the top and vents, thus creating a vacuum. And because the entire structure is raised above the water on stilts, the cool shaded air beneath is drawn up—natural air-conditioning. I have never felt overwhelmed by heat out here.

"There are some books in the armoire on the left," I said to Luz, letting an apologetic tone invade my voice. "I read a lot out here, and even if Mr. Manchester is constantly warning me that the hardbacks are going to rot in the humidity, I still keep a few at hand."

She looked up from the table at me, and I felt I had to prompt her and nodded my head at the stand-up wardrobe.

"Help yourself."

I couldn't stand the thought of watching her stare at the lantern frame all night.

She rose and went to the armoire and began browsing the piles of books on the high shelf as I kept stirring my soup. You can ruin it if you let it scald. I kept cutting looks at Luz as she carefully fingered each volume, sliding them out of their tight space, studying the covers, sometimes pulling one down and perusing the flap copy to get a sense of the story. A lot of what I kept here was Florida history, books on the wildlife of the southern United States, and travel books by Jonathan Raban, Peter Matthiessen, and Paul Theroux. I have some fiction, mostly southern stuff by Tom Franklin and some collections of Harry Crews. I was only a bit surprised when she returned to the table with a copy of Gabriel García Márquez's *Chronicle of a Death Foretold*.

"Do you like the magical realism, Mr. Freeman?" she said as I brought my warm bowl of soup to the table along with a cold Rolling Rock from the cooler.

"I liked *One Hundred Years of Solitude*," I said, recalling another García Márquez novel.

"It is better in its original Spanish," Luz said, flipping through the early pages of the novel in her hands. "But I can see how you would enjoy Mr. García's themes of solitude."

I took a long sip from the neck of the beer. Yeah, pretty obvious, I thought.

"You are not a religious man, Mr. Freeman," she said. It wasn't a question. "You are a practical man."

I nodded, an action I was using a lot lately.

"And your woman—is she practical as well?"

"My woman?" I did not recall bring Sherry's name up during any conversation with Luz Carmen.

"You told her you loved her on the phone while we were in my house."

"Yes," I said, remembering the conversation. "She is a practical person."

Luz was quiet again, looking at the pages of the novel, but not reading them.

"It's a good thing to love someone. But it is hard to do in solitude," she finally said. "You should call your woman and tell her again that you love her."

This comment was made while Luz was seemingly concentrating on reading the opening pages of the book she'd selected. I said nothing in return and finished my soup. Then I washed off the dishes at my old iron slop sink, using the old-time hand pump that drew water from below. I pulled out another beer, took my cell phone outside, and went down the steps to the small dock platform, far enough away, I thought, to keep Luz Carmen from listening in.

"Hey, how you doin'?"

"Just finished swimming. What's up?"

"I'm out at the shack."

"Yeah? Dark out there by now."

Sherry was right. This far out there is little ambient light at night, though if you know which direction to look in, you can still detect the glow of the urban world rising and then reflecting off the cloud cover. And on clear nights, if there is a moon, you can actually navigate the river in that natural luminescence.

"I'm with the client," I said.

"You think that's a good move?"

"For right now, anyway," I said, studying Sherry's question, her voice. She doesn't usually question smart tactics.

"You and a woman out in the Glades?"

Sherry is not a jealous woman. The statement caught me unawares. I was stumbling with a response and she read the hesitation.

"I'm kidding, Max."

"Oh, yeah," I said, waiting for her to continue the so-called joke by warning me not to permanently disfigure the girl while I was out here. But I said nothing.

"So I got a call from Mr. Booker," she said, breaking the uncomfortable silence.

"Yeah?"

"He wants to meet with me again."

"Progress," I said.

"Well, actually, he invited me to meet him at his home. He wants to show me some sort of classic car he's been rebuilding. Says he's thinking of adding a hand system for the accelerator and brakes; he thinks if he started driving, things might open up for him."

"Sure. A hobby—something to get back into," I said. Sherry's idea of a hobby after her amputation was physically beating herself into exhaustion on Loop Road or in the pool. "What does the sheriff's office counselor think of that?"

"I don't know, I haven't reported in yet," Sherry said. "But I think something else is up."

"Like he's making a move on you?" I said, trying to make it light, like a joke for a joke, but then regretting it instantly.

"Max."

"Sorry, babe."

"Let's not joust, OK?" she said. "I think the guy is busting to tell me something that he's holding out on."

"Like?"

"Like something to do with the accident that he's unwilling to tell anybody else. You saw the alienation going on in that gym. He's not going to spill anywhere near those meatheads. We always learned that if you get an interviewee in a place where he's comfortable, the better chance of him opening up, right?"

It was interview technique 101, but rarely happened in police work. You get them at the scene. You get them in an enclosed room downtown. You get them in a cell. But you don't often interview anyone sitting on their couch at home or out back in on their patio overlooking the garden, or in their shop tinkering with a favorite engine.

"What do you think he's holding out on?" I said. "He's been pushing the investigators on the hit-and-run, right? Wouldn't he have given them everything to help get the guy who chopped him in half?"

Again I was ruing the words the instant they left my lips, but Sherry never hesitated.

"I don't know, Max. But that's why they wanted me to work the guy, to get into his head."

"Unless they're playing you to get to the boys in the gym through him," I said, finally just tossing it out there, an angle both of us had to play since seeing McKenzie and the steroid pimples popping up on the gang in the muscle factory.

"God, that's pretty despicable."

"Which rules it out?"

"Not in the least," Sherry said.

20

JUST LISTEN TO that rumble, to that jacked-up purr, burring into your chest, vibrating your ribs. Nice, eh? That's what I'm talkin' about. Just looking at her makes me proud. The Mach 1 body style, Ram Air version; the spoiler on the back to keep that back rubber to the road; the shaker hood scoop sucking up the air to feed that sweet 428 Cobra Jet; the whole package black on red.

Yeah, you can still feel her rippling the air around you. And here you sit, in a wheelchair, poking a fucking screwdriver into the accelerator armature just to rev her. Fucking garage, man. No open road, no Alligator Alley to speed-shift her at 2:00 A.M. The car you love, and all you can do is listen to her. You are screwed, brother—all you are, is screwed.

OK, OK, maybe you shouldn't have been doing the negative vibe thing when the blonde detective came over. I mean, you did invite her, right? You called her. That was a step right there, wasn't it? Maybe you shouldn't have put it out there like you were needy, but holdin' all this shit inside is killing you. And you gotta admit it, Marty, she listened good, and knew something about where you were coming from.

So you call her and she says yes, she'll come over, but you can't take the wait, too nervous, too hyper, and too stupid for doing this in the first place. So you go where you always go now to calm down. You listen to the Mustang, chill, feel the rumble, feel a little bit alive. But it still wasn't working.

Then you saw her from inside the garage, the cab pulling up outside your place. The driver gets out and pulls her chair out of his trunk and wheels it around to the passenger-side door. You had to smile when she kind of slapped the driver's hand away from helping her. She'll do it herself, dude. This girl has her shit together; don't baby her.

You were watching from up high, your own chair rolled up onto the lifts you used to use to raise up the front end of the car to change the oil. She couldn't see you yet; the sun outside too bright, making the inside of the garage dark. She was checking out your house, the neighborhood—the whole two-bedroom middle-class thing going on here. Yeah, she probably noticed the lawn hadn't been cut for weeks, and that the front windows were carrying a film of dust, and that the hedges had gone fucking wild without a trim.

But what the hell—I'm a legless man. What do you want? So you gave the accelerator one last jack before shutting the engine down, rattling the raised garage door a little. Her head snapped around. Nice hair, catching the sun and those blue-green eyes, piercing when she looked at the place. That alone was enough for you to lose some anger. She rolled up the driveway, and you rolled down the lifts to meet her. Not exactly the Hollywood scene of the guy and girl running in the meadow to meet in some corny slow-motion embrace, but you take what you can get, right?

So you're trying to get your shit straight, be cool, be more upbeat than you are, and what does she say right off, "Hey, 1969 Mustang, right?"

I mean, what are you gonna say to a woman who knows a '69 Mustang when she sees just the ass end of one? Then she legitimately likes the car, rolls around the garage, touching the body, letting her fingers glide along the fenders, flips the chrome rings on the cable hood tie-downs. Then she asks you, actually asks you, to start the car up again, so she can listen. You swing your chair around and get the driver-side door open, and reach in to hit the ignition. We listen to the purr. Then you swing around, roll yourself up the lifts, and while she watches, you poke the accelerator arm and get that bubble of power going through the exhaust manifolds. She seems legitimately interested.

Then she starts saying something, maybe asking questions. But the noise gets in the way, so you shut the engine down again.

"You know, there's this guy down in Hollywood who had hand controls installed on his restored GTO."

You nod, but don't say anything.

"He came back from Iraq without any feet after some IED explosion wounded him—happy as a clam to be driving again."

Yeah, OK, possible, you say. But then she looks at you and gets it out of her mouth, coming straight to it, no more bullshit. "What's really bothering you, Marty? What's got a hold of you inside?"

It was that plain and simple. She asked, and you spilled, man. Don't know why. Even now you don't know why. But you tossed it all right out there and, man, if she were a plant by IA and were wearing a wire, you put it all down there on tape—stool-pigeoned on the whole gang. Fuck 'em.

Fuck me, too. I mean, how the hell did you get involved in taking deliveries of drugs from a fucking twelve-year-old kid anyway? Shit, the first time, you actually thought the other guys were just messing with you. Hey, go pick up the box from the dealer out at the Swap Shop on Sunrise. Here's the money everybody put together. And when you get there at the designated time, this kid walks right up to my Mustang and starts checking her out, staring and cooing and touching her just like the detective did.

He's saying, "Whoa, a '69 Stang! Man, that's sweet."

And you say, "Hey, great kid, but I got business here, so take off, eh?" The kid just nods his head, squeezes the box under his arm, and says, "You got the rim blow steering wheel and that teak accent stuff inside?"

He's starting to stick his head in the passenger-side window. You're like, "Hey, hey, hey, little dude, you know your cars. But I'm workin' here."

Then he backs off and holds up the box and goes, "Cool. If you don't want your merchandise, I'll just take it back home."

And fuck the guy who sent him out. Fucking Brown Man. Shit, the drug squad says they've been messing with that guy for years, say he doesn't work the streets anymore, but he's plugged into whatever anyone wants. Still, what kind of dealer sends a child out to make deliveries?

Yeah, I know—the kind who knows that a minor won't get popped as hard as an adult even if he gets caught. But shit, you even felt sorry for the kid. He loved the car, man, loved the classics as much as I had when I was his age. You actually like the kid. So why make the exchange?

Shit. You don't even know why. You fucked up again, got into it, and could have gotten out, but didn't. You made the exchange and had been making them ever since, buying up the steroids, and then turning the other way when the other shit started showing up in the box as well.

And you told all of it to her—told Sherry Richards the whole deal. I ratted them out to a pretty, one-legged detective, and you know what? Fuck 'em. It felt good.

21

IN THE MORNING, I was sitting outside on my small dock at water level when Billy called. The sun was still rising, and low beams were working their way through the veil of green.

After my conversation last night with Sherry, I'd rejoined Luz Carmen at the table and silently finished my coffee. Then I gathered a sleeping bag from my armoire and told my guest that I'd be sleeping down on the dock. It wasn't the first time I'd spent the night there. At certain times of the year, the mosquitoes are dormant and the temperature pleasant. I like the openness of the air. I like to stare up at the tree canopy and watch stars slip in and out of the foliage. That wasn't my motivation last night. With a woman client upstairs, I told myself I was being a professional. Maybe sometime in the future, I'd tell Sherry the same thing.

Billy's call had come while I'd still been dozing.

"My ballistics guy says it probably came from a pistol with a suppressor attached. He based that on the lack of extensive powder burns on the animal's scalp," Billy said.

"You have a ballistics guy?"

"I took photos of the bullet removed during the necropsy and passed them on to an expert, Max."

"And the original went to the Palm Beach Sheriff's Office?"

"Of course," Billy said. "We are cooperating one hundred percent with the authorities."

"They could trace it with a comparison," I said. "Maybe get lucky."

"Yes. If they expedite it, they might come up with something in a year or two."

Again, that cynicism in Billy's voice—that's usually my way of talking. But we both know how swamped and understaffed crime labs are. No one in the business watches the popular TV shows without scoffing at how they depict results that magically pop up instantaneously.

"Anything else with the dog?" I said.

"Like?"

"Well, maybe it had a wallet in its mouth along with a chunk of butt flesh?"

"No such luck, Max. But that breed is known to clamp down and never let go. I wouldn't doubt if Fido got in a bite. You saw how silent and sneaky the beast was. We can turn the dog's remains over to the sheriff along with our theory. They might take some blood samples from its mouth, but again . . ."

"Yeah, by next year," I said.

As we spoke, I became aware of a subtle movement to my right. I did not turn my head, and looked only by cutting my eyes in that direction. A tricolored heron about two feet tall was just yards away, stalking the shallow water for baitfish. The eye on my side of its head wandered, but I can never tell what direction a bird is looking. This one's bill was long and tapered, like an old woman's knitting needle, and its wings, neck, and head were slate blue. A white line ran the length of its throat. It raised one orange-colored foot and then froze, like a dancer, balanced for a strike or for a sudden leap in the choreography. Billy's and my conversation had stopped, and the silence seemed to have frozen us all.

"How is Ms. Carmen?" Billy finally asked.

"Upstairs," I answered. Suddenly, as if I had been directing the bird alone, there was a flutter and then a big *whoosh* of wing and air and the utterance of a harsh *GAWK* as the heron rose and pirouetted gracefully through an opening in the trees, and vanished.

"She's fine," I said, looking up through the now empty hole in the canopy. "Safe."

"Can she stand it for a couple of days while I keep pushing the feds for some protective custody? This proof that someone shot the dog and that same someone probably set off the explosion should crank up the pressure."

I turned my head to the doorway up the stairs above me. "I don't know, Billy. I'll have to ask her."

"Be convincing, Max."

Convincing someone to stay isolated in the middle of nowhere is mostly determined by whether that someone has an affinity for being alone. I discovered the ability in myself by crawling into books when I was young, disappearing into worlds I'd never seen, reading conversations between people I would never meet, absorbing life lessons through characters overcoming odds I would most likely never face. I used the ability as a refuge, taking a book and a flashlight under my covers as a kid while my drunk and violent father bounced my mother off the walls downstairs in the middle of the night. I wiped tears from my eyes and read the pages, trying to escape with Huck Finn or walk a new beach on Treasure Island while the muffled gasps and sharp curses ricocheted up the stairwell.

But Luz Carmen's brother was dead, and I had not seen her shed a tear. She had not yet claimed his body. She might hide, but the reality was not going away.

I stepped quietly up the stairs, and when I opened the door to the shack, my eyes went immediately to the sunlight sifting through the east window. Luz had figured out how to adjust the Bahama shutters and was raised up in the bottom bunk of the bed, reading. She met my look and nodded a good morning.

"Coffee?" I said, moving to reload the stove with wood, and then start the fire.

"Yes, please."

"Did you sleep?"

"Did you?"

I rinsed and then filled my tin coffeepot with water.

"Some," I said. "It was a little cool."

"The heat rises," she said. And when I looked over, she was still looking at the book, her knees up, acting as a platform.

I scooped coffee into the small, one-legged basket, and then lowered it into the pot. I washed the cover after removing the small glass percolator bubble, and then remounted it. I opened a lid on the stove top and set the pot over the open flame.

"I can make some oatmeal," I said, pulling a chair out from the table. From here, I could see that Luz Carmen was still fully dressed. She'd slept in her clothes, as had I.

"I want to see my brother," she said, finally letting the book slide down into her lap.

"I know," I said, and then recounted Billy's morning message—that the dog had been killed by a gunman. "They'll most likely want to do an autopsy now on your brother's body. They'll probably assign homicide now. They'll start working it harder, faster."

Luz took in the information without reaction, staring ahead at some vision all her own. But the filtered sun caught the moisture on her cheeks and glistened. "I killed my own brother," she said, the words coming out of her mouth even though I couldn't even see that her lips had moved.

"If you play along, and if you keep your mouth shut. If you simply work and keep your head down and see nothing, you live," she said. Her voice was not whiny or complaining, but stilted and rote and without emotion. "My brother would be alive if not for me."

Billy and I have had this conversation deep into many nights on his balcony facing the sea: Is the man who sits by and ignores the criminality taking place in his sight as complicit as the man doing the crime? What about the Germans who watched the camp trains being loaded with Jews, or the Iraqi citizens who saw the roadside bomb being planted and turned the other way? Not to mention the Wall Street underlings who shook their heads and zipped their lips when they knew the bundled mortgages would never pass muster?

I was not up for a debate with a grieving woman. I stayed silent for a long time.

"I need to bury my brother," Luz said.

"You will," I told her.

By early afternoon, I had replaced a rotting plank of wood on the port side of my dock, freed up a jammed window sash, fixed a hole in a screen that looked like it had been plucked open by an animal—rodent, bird, or reptile based on its size, the meticulous snipping, and random uselessness. I'd also finished the first quarter of Peter Matthiessen's *Shadow Country*, a Florida history lesson unparalleled.

Luz Carmen staked out a spot down on the dock. Apparently, she'd finished the English-language version of *Chronicle of a Death Foretold* and was starting on my paperback copy of *All Quiet on the Western Front,* which she must have dug out of the back of the armoire while I was sleeping outside. Her choice of reading material while grieving over a dead brother was not mine to ponder, but I do have an innate problem with people who can read so damn fast. How do they do it without missing the subtleties, innuendo, and small word gems that authors sweat through and take days of writing and rewriting to achieve? It seems both cheating, and self-cheating.

But I am a slow reader, and it's probably just jealousy. I read slowly. I write slowly, and none too poetically considering that most of my experience has been filling out incident reports as a cop and now writing up surveillance narratives for Billy. When I stole glances at Luz, I noted that every once in a while she would look up from the book and stare out into the green of the river forest.

What was in her mind's eye was hers alone. I thought of the advice shrinks give, that people shouldn't be alone at times of great loss. But who isn't alone with their thoughts? You handle them your own way, and hopefully grow stronger. Closure is bullshit. In the absence of some kind of biological memory wipe, there is no such thing. Personal loss is always with us. We learn to live with it; we don't make it go away.

I was about to interrupt Luz for a late lunch when my cell phone rang.

"Mr. Freeman, this is Dan, over at the ranger station."

"Yeah?"

"I just wanted to give you a heads-up that Joey finished with your truck and dropped it by here. So it's in the parking lot."

"Great, Dan. Thanks. I appreciate it," I said, wondering what the hell the real reason for the call was. Dan had been around long enough to know that when I was at the shack I often didn't make contact with him or anyone else for days or weeks at a time. He wouldn't call with something as minor as my truck being dropped off.

"What else, Dan?"

"Uh, well, I wanted to let you know there was somebody messing around near your Gran Fury early this morning, just around daybreak. I was up, and I keep an eye out. When I saw the guy, I scared him off with my big beam flashlight." The ranger had started out with reticence, as if he didn't want to be the one giving me bad news. Now his words were running as fast as he could get them out.

"He scrambled the hell out of there fast. I looked over the car this morning; it doesn't look like he got it open or anything like that—no scratches or nothing. Probably just some kid, you know, looking for an unlocked car to steal change and stuff out of."

I let him stumble through the whole explanation, do his duck and cover before responding. I went inside the shack out of hearing range of Luz Carmen and closed the door.

"OK, Dan, did you get any kind of look at this guy—race, size, clothing, or distinguishing tattoos?" I said, tossing the tattoo thing in there to goose him a little and remind him that I was, after all, an ex-cop.

"Uh, yeah, well, black guy in dark, maybe black clothes, with long sleeves. He was uh, probably under, like, five ten. Kinda skinny."

"Carrying anything, Dan?" I said, moving him along step by step. Witnesses don't always get their memory pictures focused until you put a frame around them. "When he scrambled away, do you recall him carrying anything?"

"Yeah, you know, he was carrying some kind of package under his arm. But I checked the car, Mr. Freeman, and I don't think he got inside. It was still all locked up, and there was no damage, you know?"

I was walking circles around the table, setting up the scene in my own head.

"And he was kinda limping."

"What?"

"When I told you he was scrambling away, it was more like he was crab walking. I remember thinking he wasn't like, sprinting or anything, when I got the light on him. He was more like trying to stay low, but pulling a leg behind."

"OK, Dan, that's good—that's the kind of thing I need. Did he have a hat on? Was something covering his head, his hair?"

"Uh, no. But he was dirty."

"Explain."

"The light picked up the grass and stuff on his back—like maybe he was under the car, hot-wiring it or something."

You don't hot-wire a car from underneath. From underneath, you're either changing the oil, or sabotaging the damn thing.

"And you said this all happened early this morning?" I asked.

"Yeah, at daybreak."

"And you're calling me now, at two P.M., to tell me my truck was delivered?"

I was trying not to get angry with the guy, and ask what the hell took him so long. After all, he had no idea what I was into, the safe-keeping of Luz Carmen or the threats. I never tell the innocent people on the periphery of my life about what I do. People get crazy enough with all the out of proportion crime news they see on television. It's that contextual half-truth that hurts them, not the real stuff they'll never know about.

"I'm sorry, Mr. Freeman. You know, I just thought if you had a lady friend out there, you wouldn't want to be disturbed."

A lady friend . . .

"It's all right, Dan. Thanks for calling. I'll be in soon," I said, and punched off the cell.

I recalled a quote I picked up somewhere: "Great minds discuss ideas; average minds discuss events; small minds discuss people."

Was I being talked about? Hell with it, I didn't give a shit. I stepped outside and called down to Luz Carmen.

"Pack up. We gotta go."

22

I WAS STANDING where Dan said he'd been when he saw the man messing with the Gran Fury. I was trying to re-create the smoky light of predawn in my head; how good a look could the ranger have managed? The distance was maybe thirty yards. There is little ambient light out here at night. But when Dan showed me the big Inova T3 flashlight he used for spotting poachers and night fishermen, and for checking the occasional snarl of a bobcat, I had to figure he got a decent look. The high-intensity beam can throw 150 lumens at someone 300 feet away. No wonder the ranger saw flecks of dry grass on the prowler's back.

My own truck, newly washed and polished, was parked in front of the car, but I kept my focus on the Gran Fury, as if it were a suspect.

First I got my truck keys from Dan and carefully backed the F-150 away. Only then did I approach the Gran Fury to begin an inspection, searching the grass around it first, looking for any kind of obvious disturbance. Then without touching the car, I peered in all the windows, carefully looking at the door handles and what I could see of the steering column, to determine whether the visitor had actually been inside before Dan lit him up. The hood was locked down with no sign of tampering. The doors were tight—nothing.

I got down on the ground from the side of the car opposite from the ranger station, figuring the guy would have done the same, using the car body as a shield. I used Dan's light to illuminate the undercarriage, starting from the front—no out-of-place wires. No signs of unusual connections to the engine. I moved the light back a bit. The front wheels and brake lines looked undisturbed. Back further, there was no indication the bottom edges of the front doors were scratched, and there was nothing like a pressure switch attached to them. I ran the light over the oil pan and the driveshaft and then to the back wheels. On the nearest rocker arm, I found it. The sight of the gray-colored package made me blanch. I think I actually held the light on it for a full minute, frozen, no panic, but frozen.

If you'd expect to find several red sticks of dynamite strapped together with an alarm clock taped to it, you'd be disappointed. Instead, I was staring at an innocuous form about the size of a one-pound box of Arm & Hammer Pure Baking Soda. It was wrapped in some kind of thin cellophane like Saran Wrap and attached to the axle near the gas tank with several turns of duct tape. I didn't slide away. I didn't breathe.

After some time, I actually had a fleeting thought about the heat from the light that I couldn't seem to move off the object. Don't be stupid, I thought: Heat doesn't set off explosives; electricity or a fuse does. That made me focus. I searched the brick of plastic for some form of detonator. If someone wanted to kill me with a remote detonator, wouldn't he have done it by now while my head was under the car? Nice logic, Max. Feel better? No.

I squirmed and shifted my body to get a look at the other side of the package. It wasn't wired as far as I could tell. Only then did I worm my way back out. I stood and took a deep breath—was that the first breath I'd taken since I saw the block of explosive? Then I walked back to the ranger station where I'd asked Luz Carmen to stay.

"We need to get you under federal protection," I said.

She just nodded, as if had asked her to go to the corner grocery for bread. Dan was looking at the side of my face when I turned to him.

"You need to call the sheriff and tell them to get a bomb squad out here," I said, trying to sound calm. "Somebody strapped the car with an explosive, but it doesn't look like they had the chance to put a detonator on it. But we can't take a chance."

If there was a bomber still waiting out there for Luz to get into the vicinity of the car, he wasn't going to get much satisfaction. Maybe Dan had scared the guy off before he had the chance to finish rigging the thing. The way the explosive was taped to the rocker arm, it wouldn't have been a matter of just grabbing the thing and running when the flashlight beam hit him. So he left it behind and ran. But an attempt had been made. It might even be an easy task to simply remove the package, but I wasn't going to do it.

Dan turned to the phone on his desk without hesitation. But after dialing the number, I caught him looking at me with wide eyes as he tried to process what I'd just told him so he could reword it to the dispatcher. Bomb. Explosive. This was not a skill set he'd learned in park ranger school. While he was waiting for the connection, I went out onto the porch and called Billy.

"I'll call the bomb squad immediately," was Billy's first response.

"Being done."

"And Ms. Carmen?"

"Sitting right here. Quiet."

"I'm calling the feds as soon as we hang up," Billy said with anger in his voice, which is rare but was becoming more prevalent. He is not a man who likes to be put off; yet he usually reacts by requesting higher-ups, and then dropping the names of prominent executives, judges, and politicians. Though Billy isn't the type to get mad, he does get things done.

After we hung up, I stood looking out onto the wide river in front of me, the flat water ruffled by an eastern breeze. You could tell by the subtle brush back of the ripples that the bulk of the water was moving one way, while the opposing wind nipped at it in futility. The tide was going out. We were close enough now to the ocean that the pull of gravity was working its wonder. Nature does not give up her pull, despite what piddling man, even Al Gore himself, does. We will not destroy the world. The world will go on even after we've destroyed ourselves.

People won't stop doing what they do, either. It's inside us. Someone out there housed a predator inside, and it was leaking out. He wasn't a pro. But this time, his work wasn't going to look like an accident, as it had at the mobile home. The signature of explosive would be distinctive, if that was indeed what was in the package. Our assassin was running out of ideas, or was just plain getting anxious and sloppy.

Who was he—an amateur? A wannabe—an ambitious young one? But who gives the ambitious amateur the targets? Motivation is all, Max. Who wants to kill you or Luz Carmen, or both?

From a distance, I heard the sound of sirens, then the distinctive deep *honk! honk!* of a rescue or fire vehicle coming from the direction of the park entrance to the north. I knew there wasn't much use for the display, but when the bomb squad gets a call out, the bells and whistles come with it.

A sheriff's car was the first one into the parking lot, followed by the bomb squad's utility truck, and sure enough, a fire engine—and lastly, a paramedic unit. People who question what they see as an overreaction would also be the first ones to bitch and second-guess if there wasn't enough backup to handle their own emergency.

Dan and Luz Carmen joined me on the porch. The deputy from the cop car went straight to Dan, given that he was the guy in the ranger uniform. Dan explained the situation again, a bit better now that he'd had time to edit himself. When he used the phrase *Mr. Freeman's car,* he nodded at me. Now I drew the spotlight and the scrutiny.

Since we were looking at the Gran Fury from a distance as we spoke, the officer in charge of bomb unit figured it out pretty quickly and began unloading equipment. After spelling out for the deputy that I'd been told someone suspicious was seen near the car in early darkness, I explained that I'd carefully checked out the periphery of the car without touching it and had indeed looked underneath and observed the package, but no obvious triggering device.

The deputy wasn't stupid. When he caught me using the words *periphery* and *observed,* he interjected.

"Are you in law enforcement, Mr. Freeman?"

"Was."

He looked into my eyes, waiting.

"I was a cop in Philadelphia. I'm a PI now, working for an attorney in West Palm Beach."

"I see," he said, not bothering to elaborate on what exactly he was now thinking. "And you, ma'am?"

Luz Carmen looked at him with the blank expression that both legal and illegal aliens have honed to perfection in South Florida.

"She is a client," I said. "You might want to get in touch with a Sergeant Lynch concerning a trailer fire two days ago. I think this could all tie in together."

The deputy nodded. "One thing at a time, Mr. Freeman," he said, and then turned to the bomb squad sergeant who had joined our group. "Can you explain again, in as much detail as possible, what you've already observed around and under the car to Sergeant Peters here? I'll make some calls."

I did my best for the sergeant and two of his men, and then watched as the entire gang got together, working out their plan of approach. The fire engine was repositioned, its hoses placed at the ready. The paramedics turned their ambulance around, either to have the back doors ready for any emergency admission, or to haul ass if something went boom. Then everyone on the four-man bomb and arson unit pulled on the ubiquitous surgical gloves and began to circle around the Gran Fury. They started some fifteen yards out, and in time I could see them tightening the grid.

It was a probe-and-poke routine, not unlike what I had done myself two hours ago. At one point, a member raised his hand. He was about ten yards from the car, waist-high in grasses. When he called out something, the sergeant joined him. They were behind the Gran Fury, in the direction Dan had told them the prowler had fled. They bent and disappeared under my sightline.

When he finally stood, the sergeant called out an order I couldn't hear, and the entire team moved in on the car, this time less tactically, more aggressively. Within thirty minutes, Sergeant Peters came back to the porch, the loosened package of explosive in one gloved hand. In the other, he carefully held what looked like a dismantled garage door opener; his thumb tip at one corner, his index finger at the other.

He did not look me in the face when he said: "I'm not sure it would have worked, but there's no reason why not. But it seems our bomber didn't have the time to plant the detonator and use this as a remote switch." He held up the garage door opener. "All you need is a current to pass between two contacts."

Then he looked up. "You were still damn lucky, Mr. Freeman."

I agreed without saying so.

"If you don't mind my asking, Sergeant," I said, "what kind of expertise does it take to hook up something like this?"

"Tough part is getting the explosives. They're still near impossible to get even on the black market. But the firing device can be anything: cell phones, pagers, toy car remotes. Hell, I was in Iraq for eight months with my National Guard unit; children over there know how to rig these things."

Again I thought of the propane tank at the end of the mobile home: a thimble of C-4; a toy car remote, for Christ's sake.

"If you have your keys, sir, my guys will take a look inside," he said. "You all should probably still stay here though, just in case."

I handed over the keys, and while his squad did their thing, the sergeant went to his van and returned with a cardboard box. He was still holding the garage door opener carefully between his fingers.

Again, he addressed Dan as the person in charge. "May we use your office, Ranger? I need an electrical plug."

"Yeah, sure," Dan said, and opened the door. He followed, intrigued as much as I was. We all went inside.

The sergeant put the box on Dan's desk and traced the lamp cord down to a wall socket. He took a simple coffee cup warmer out of the box, set it on the edge of the desk, and plugged it in.

I knew what was coming, but watched anyway.

"One of the problems with collecting evidence is that a lot of departments say they don't have equipment and lab time," the sergeant said, taking a grocery store roll of aluminum foil out of the box and a small tube of what I soon figured out was superglue.

The sergeant set the coffee cup warmer in one corner of the now-empty box. Then he took a piece of aluminum foil and formed it into a kind of ashtray, setting it on top of the coffee warmer where the cup would usually go. After opening the tube of superglue, he put a glob about the size of a nickel on the aluminum foil.

Dan was narrowing his eyebrows and looking over at me when the sergeant asked for a cup of hot coffee.

"Uh, yeah," he said. "I just started a fresh pot this morning?"

The sergeant took a full cup from Dan and set it inside the box.

"It adds some humidity to the air," he said. Dan just stared.

The sergeant then placed the garage door opener inside the box, carefully leaning it into a corner on its edges so that every flat surface was exposed. He then ripped off another piece of aluminum foil. We watched while he rubbed his finger on the side of his nose and pressed it to the small piece of foil, and then leaned it against a wall inside the box.

"A control standard," I said.

The sergeant looked up. "You really were a cop, Mr. Freeman."

I just shrugged.

He closed the top flaps of the box and said, "Be about ten minutes. If we get some good prints, we'll send them off to the lab. I've just seen too many guys put these things in a plastic evidence bag and mess them up in transport."

"You're a careful man, Sergeant," I said, and he stared at me with a "duh, yeah?" look on his face. He defuses bombs for a living, Freeman, whatta ya think?

Back outside, Luz Carmen was sitting in an old wooden straight-backed chair on the porch, staring out at the river, seemingly paying no attention to the bomb techs who had now opened all four doors of the Gran Fury, and appeared to be searching the interior. I went down on one knee next to her.

"Ms. Carmen," I said. "I need you to call your friend, the woman at the beach house. Do you remember her saying that she noticed a black man out in front of the Royal Flamingo Villas, a man who scared her?"

Luz Carmen nodded.

"I need to ask her if she can describe him in more detail," I said. "I need you to ask her if the man was limping when she saw him."

I handed her my cell phone and stood up. I was now thinking about Dan's description of the man he spooked while the guy was rigging an explosive to blow us both to hell. I had no doubt that the bomb squad sergeant would turn up a viable print on the garage door opener if the guy had been stupid enough to handle the trigger with his bare hands. But now I was wondering how the hell he would have found us. Had he followed us from the Royal Flamingo Villas? If so, I was pissed I'd allowed that to happen.

While Luz talked in Spanish on the cell phone, I watched as the bomb squad began to abandon the car, closing the doors roughly, an indication, I figured, that all was clear.

One of the squad members walked up to me holding a small black object the size of a beeper.

"The car is absolutely clean, Mr. Freeman," he said, handing over my keys. "But we did find this under the passenger seat."

He held up the object between two fingers, just as the sergeant had with the garage opener. "It's a GPS tracker, the kind they use on delivery truck fleets to track where the vehicle is at all times. Mean anything to you?"

I was looking at the tracker, thinking about the Gran Fury. Had it ever been parked unlocked where someone would have had access? Sure, they could have popped the old locks without leaving an obvious sign, but had anyone been inside other than me? Who the hell had put a GPS in it, and why? Then I remembered the admirer, saw the vision of a child running his fingertips over the chrome; I recalled inviting the kid to go ahead, climb inside. I'd actually given him permission.

"It means I'm an idiot," I said, and the officer raised his eyebrows. "You'd better go in and give it to your sergeant to process, but I'm pretty sure he's not going to find a ten-year-old's prints on file to match them."

After the tech took the evidence inside the ranger's office, I stood on the porch, trying to retrace all of my steps ever since I'd talked to the Brown Man and his son in their Fort Lauderdale neighborhood. Luz Carmen stepped up to hand back my cell phone.

"Yes, she thinks she remembers a man," she said. "He was black, and maybe twenty years old, very carefully dressed. She noticed because he didn't look like he belonged at the beach. And when she looked back to see if he would follow her, he was walking away with a limp."

Same as Dan's daybreak suspect, our bomber, our tracker. He didn't have to follow because he knew exactly where we were going and where we'd been: northwest Fort Lauderdale, the trailer park, the Royal Flamingo Villas, right here at the boat ramp, and Sherry's home. Jesus, Sherry's—he'd tracked me to a cop's house.

I thought of my gun—still in the shack, wrapped up in oilcloth. Even if I took Dan's Boston Whaler, it would take more than an hour to get out there and back.

"I gotta go," I told Luz. "Stay here until Mr. Manchester gets here. Stay here with these officers." I went for the Gran Fury instead of my truck. The Gran Fury would be faster; the spotlights might help clear the way.

The firefighters and paramedics just watched as I fired up the Gran Fury and sped past them, spitting dust and gravel. They looked at one another and at the door to the shack, probably wondering why the cops were letting me drive the car away. I might have heard someone holler "Hey!" when I looked in the rearview and saw the sergeant standing on the porch, watching my bumper.

23

I WAS DRIVING like an idiot for the second time in a week. This time, I was avoiding rear-end collisions instead of perpetuating them. The only saving grace was that the evening rush hour on I-95 was ebbing. I had both spotlights aimed forward and glaring. My headlights were on bright, and I used the horn only when I needed to zoom around someone who wouldn't get over.

I stayed at eighty m.p.h. most of the way through Palm Beach County until the inevitable snags off West Palm, and then gunned it up again in Broward, with slow downs off Deerfield and Pompano Beaches. I kept dialing Sherry's cell and kept getting the recorded message. She'd ditched the house phone years ago.

My mother used to ring the house phone in our old South Philly home at night when we were away. "I only let it ring a couple of times, and then hang up," she'd explain. "That way the burglars think someone's home and is picking up."

My drunk father thought she was nuts. "Buy a fucking dog," he'd say.

"They shoot dogs, don't they?" she'd respond.

"So arm him."

This was a typical exchange: family life at the Freemans'.

But Sherry would be armed; she's a cop. Still, the MO of the guy who was making my stomach churn and my head grind was not the kind that had standoffs and faced up to those he intended to kill. He was the kind that set off a propane tank explosion while you were asleep. He was the kind that put a bomb under your car, waiting in the weeds to blow you to hell with a garage opener. He was the kind that might work for a notorious drug dealer who was trying to get rid of all witnesses and connections to his "expanded" operations in Medicare fraud and the prescription drug trade.

The only person who I could recall having access to my Gran Fury to plant the tracking device was the Brown Man's son, the fascinated kid I let climb into the passenger seat while I was trying to rattle his father's cage. If the former street dealer had set one of his other protégés on to Andrés and Luz Carmen, and by extension to me, then we were being stalked. And considering the methods of the stalker and clues he'd left in his wake, he wasn't the sharpest knife in the drawer.

But a wannabe hit man can be as dangerous as the barely believable Hollywood types you see in movies. And as Baghdad's bombers taught us all, they don't give a damn about collateral damage to innocents.

When I got through to Billy on his cell, I told him I'd left Luz at the ranger's station with a dozen cops and firefighters. He said he was already en route with a federal witness protection agent. I gave him an abbreviated rundown on the bombing attempt, while I *whooshed* around three minivans pulling some sort of convoy in the inside lane. I wished I had the old Whelen rumbler police siren that came with the original Gran Fury to rattle their windows.

"Any idea who this guy is?" Billy asked.

"The sheriff's office will know as soon as they run that print, but I'm not waiting around," I said. "If he's stupid enough to be blowing up witnesses, he's stupid enough to try and set up something at Sherry's."

I tossed the cell in the passenger seat just as I came up on the Broward Boulevard exit and passed the waiting lines in the side lane. Then I cut everyone off with a wide and illegal turn east. I knew this was the fastest route and would also take me past the Fort Lauderdale Police Headquarters. If I was lucky, doing twice the speed limit in front of the cops would get me a tail, and I'd lead them all to Sherry's house and explain later.

It didn't work that way. When I rolled into the neighborhood, I was alone, and doused my headlights. Sherry's car appeared to be untouched and covered. The house windows were dark. I parked one driveway up the street and got out. It was just past twilight, and Victoria Park was the essence of a quaint and quiet place, inhabited by working folks, some singles, some families who got in when real estate was low, and then held on when the property taxes started climbing.

There was a car parked on the street a block north. Most people who were home were in their own driveways, so the Jeep Cherokee stuck out. I memorized the plate number and then thought: paranoid Max. But still, I went around the house, not using any of the usual entrances, the gate to the backyard, or the front door. I stopped at the side fence, and listened.

First thing wrong: The pool motor was off. Not just the motor that creates the hard current for Sherry to swim against, but the regular skimmer motor that ran constantly. The underwater lights were on. I could see the aqua glow reflecting high in the oak tree. I eased down the property line to the back where Sherry had installed just a thigh-high wire fence that blended into the ficus hedge. Through the leaves I could see the raised deck, the French doors to her bedroom, the sliders that led into the kitchen—nothing.

I was starting to embarrass myself, casing my own girlfriend's house, when I picked up the movement at the pool-side motor stand. Something black slipping out of the shadow—the hump of a man's back and the movement of arms.

The motor stand is about the size of a small doghouse, and my visitor was on the far side, bent where the electrical circuit box opens, seemingly preoccupied. I slipped off my shoes, and then moved barefooted as quietly as I could along the backside of the hedge. The neighbors had recently mowed their Saint Augustine lawn, giving me a cushion of spiky grass that poked at the bottoms of my feet, but muted any noise. At the corner, where the hedge meets the opposite fence, I stopped and evaluated. I was maybe eight yards away from the motor stand, as close as possible without coming out into the open.

I watched and listened, my night sight gaining efficiency. My hearing focused. I heard the scrape of metal on metal, and the slight echoing clink of something being dropped into, what, a pan?

A maintenance guy? Not at 7:00 P.M. And there was no truck out front. The regular pool guy drives a pickup with one of those little trailers in back that holds vacuum hoses and yellow bottles of chlorine. As I watched, a figure appear over the stand, the aqua light illuminated only the underside of his chin, shadowed his eyes. He was black, with a thin build. It looked like he was wearing a watch cap—in Florida, eighty degrees, and humid? He was no maintenance guy.

He came around the pump stand, staying low, moved to my side, and crouched again. I could see that he was dragging his right leg, and now had to extend it behind him to bend and reach down into the water above one of the submerged pool lights. A dog bite will do that to a hamstring.

I felt the adrenaline hit me again. I was pissed, but had to fight the anger. This asshole was trying to booby-trap my girl's pool. I took three deep silent breaths and did the scenario in my head: over the thigh-high fence, through a weak spot in the ficus, eight yards to the crouched figure. If he's armed, he'll hear me coming and shoot me before I make five yards. He took the dog out with a silenced pistol. I breathed again, felt around me with my palms.

On the ground were a gaggle of hard half-inch berries. The back neighbor had planted a wild olive tree in the corner. Maybe he thought he was going to use them in his martini, but down here, the berries fall when they're still hard. I needed a diversion, and the old ways are often the best simply because they work.

I grabbed up a handful of berries, then carefully raised one foot to gain purchase on the top crossbar of the fence. My true target was half-lying on the apron of the pool, both hands doing something in the water. I leaned back, and like a WWII infantryman lobbing a grenade, I looped a handful of the berries into the air over the hedge, hoping the arc would carry them to Sherry's deck. While they were still airborne, I mounted the fence. When the fusillade of berries rattled down on the wooden planks of the deck, I exploded through the leaves.

The man only made it to one knee, his head turning first to the deck noise, then to me as I burst through the ficus. I made two long strides and launched myself, head first like a spear, arms spread wide like a linebacker, and met him shoulder high.

My momentum carried us both into the water, where my fingers went straight for the guy's face. Go for the eyes, make him panic.

We twisted together, slower in the water than we would have been on land, soaked clothes pulling us down and deterring any quick blows. The heel of the man's hand came up under my chin, a classic defensive move, but the slickness of water made it easy to dislodge. He tried kicking with his feet, shoes dragging, bereft of velocity. I couldn't get my fingers in his eye sockets and went for the head. The watch cap was long gone. I got a handful of hair and yanked back and down.

I was a good swimmer. Sherry had always been amazed how long I could hold my breath when we used to go reef snorkeling. With a fistful of hair, I took the guy to the bottom with me. He tried to punch me in the throat, but again the movement was slowed by the water. This wasn't the street, or a karate dojo. I kicked my bare feet, got behind him, and rode his back toward the bottom. In the deep end, Sherry's pool was only eight feet. I'd gone down several times to clear the bottom suction drain of big oak leaves. Sometimes I'd empty my lungs of air and just sit down here, looking up at the sun rippling at the surface. On those occasions, I felt I could stay down here for days.

My adversary was not made of the same stuff. I could feel his struggle weakening, his arms going limp. I could actually hear the bubbles of oxygen leaving his throat. Maybe he was screaming, or begging. I couldn't tell. I hadn't opened my eyes since diving forward off the fence.

When we made the surface, I heard a gasp. It was mine. I opened my throat and my eyes at the same time and started stroking to the shallow end, dragging a shirt collar in my hand. The man had gone full limp, and when I got to the point I could stand, I drew him near. He was face-up in the water. I pushed my fingers into the side of his cheeks, pried open his jaws, and pulled his head back so his throat was in a straight line. As soon as his airway was open, a huge gurgling intake of breath went into the vacuum and then came back out sputtering.

"What the fuck, man? What the . . ."

Consciousness came back when the air started going in and out. I was still jacked up with adrenaline. I pulled back hard again on his hair. "Ah, ah, ah," he yelled.

I took an arm up behind his back, putting some pressure on the shoulder joint when I felt muscle function coming back to him. I determined the guy was in his mid-twenties, maybe 150, 160 pounds. I had him in bulk and height, a distinct advantage now that I had my feet solidly on the bottom of the pool in chest-deep water.

"Who are you, and why the fuck are you here?" I growled into the guy's ear, turning his head a bit with the twist of hair in my fist.

"I ain't nobody, man, nobody."

"That's good. We start with the truth," I said, using the arm bar and the hank of hair, plunging his head back into the water. He shook and reached back to claw me with his free hand to no avail. I let him bubble for a few second, just to remind the memory cells of oxygen deprava-tion, and then brought him back up.

"Again—who are you, and why are you here?"

Phlegm was now drooling out of the guy's mouth. He was back to spitting and coughing. He truly did not like the water. "OK, man, OK. It's just a job, man."

"A job? What the hell do you mean, a job?" I said, and could feel the astonishment in my own voice. "You came to fuck with my girlfriend's home as a job?" I could feel my hand twisting tighter in the guy's hair, pulling some of it out. I could feel my forearm ratcheting up his elbow; tendons would start popping soon.

"What? You've got a contract or something out on her? You do the same thing to the kids in the mobile home, kill them on contract? You set up the kid before that, try to gun him down with your gangbanger buddies? You try to blow me up in my car and take out a woman wit-ness as well?"

The guy was twisting his head a different way now, a way to indicate an answer rather than trying to get free. "I don't run with no bangers.

I work alone, man," he said, taking deep breaths, but getting the words out clear, almost taking time to be prideful of what he was saying.

"What, you're some kind of assassin, some kind of contract killer?"

He waited before answering, just long enough to make my fingers flex again and my muscles tense for another dunking. "I'm a professional, man. I don't do no drive-by shit. That's for punks."

"Oh, a professional," I said, the sarcasm legitimate. "That's why I'm here to drown your sorry ass because you professionally fucked up your little bomb trick. That's why you're trying to mess with a woman cop who has nothing to do with any of the rest of them, because you're such a professional?"

Letting anger get the best of me, I plunged the guy's head back down into the water and put my knee in the middle of his back. The bubbles rose. The squirming became violent. I considered, twice, drowning him. It wasn't exactly water boarding, but it was on the same level.

This time when he came up, his eyes were wide and his mouth was like a gasping fish. "OK, man," he coughed. "I didn't know she was a cop. I didn't know. I knew the other one was a cop, but not this one, man."

I was concentrating on the phrase *I knew the other one was a cop, but not this one* when I saw blue-and-red lights filtering through the low tree bows and bushes. They were coming without sirens. Someone had called.

"What other one?" I yelled into the man's ear. "What other cop?"

"The dude on the highway, Mr. Muscle Man sheriff's deputy. Carlyle said that one had to go like an accident and that's my thing, you know. I make it look like an accident 'cause I'm a professional."

I stared into the water, deciphering what I'd just heard. The guy was actually giving his damn résumé.

"Pinched that motherfucker off, man," he said, somehow putting braggadocio into his wet voice. "Made him scream like a girl."

I punched the guy in the back of the head just as the first officer came through Sherry's back gate. My knuckles snapped and mister professional asshole went out like a light. I dragged him unconscious to the stairs and up onto the pool apron as the officer on scene was holstering his gun.

The wannabe assassin was still breathing, though. I don't know why I let him.

24

SHERRY AND I sat next to each other in the dark on her deck. She'd come in with the second wave of cops through the back gate after I had already pulled the electrical breaker feeding the pool and pump and porch lights, just to be safe. She had wheeled herself up onto the deck and watched as officers scoured her home and yard, considering it a crime scene and—after a quick rundown from me—an attempted attack on one of their own.

After officers hauled the would-be assassin away, the sergeant on duty asked me to sit and wait while he went through the evidence left behind. The intruder's satchel near the pump stand held a small metal toolbox containing splicing pliers, waterproof electrical tape, wire crimpers, and bolt cutters. Lying on top of the bag was a Beretta 92FS loaded with fifteen rounds of 147-grain ammunition. The factory barrel was threaded and a suppressor was screwed onto the end.

The serial numbers on the gun had been melted off with acid, but I told the sergeant that my attorney had a slug obtained during a necropsy of a pit bull at a mobile home firebombing scene in Palm Beach County. I added that the slug would most likely match up with the ballistics on the Beretta he now had in his hand. The sergeant looked at me, turned to Sherry, and without emotion said, "Shit, this isn't going to be a simple breaking and entering, is it?"

Then I answered questions for more than an hour while Fort Lauderdale Police crime scene officers went over the pool, the pump stand, and the back fence. Their quick conclusion was that whoever the supposed assassin was, he'd been trying to rig the electrical feed to the pump with a spliced wire that he'd intended to route into the water, thus setting up an electrocution of anyone diving into the pool for a daily swim. It might have worked, they said. Or it just might have shorted out the whole system as soon as anyone turned on the pump.

"Would the suspect know anything about your swimming habits?" the sergeant taking notes asked us. I looked at Sherry and even in the dim light of the houselights could see that flicker of green in her eyes that always means she's pissed.

"Was some asshole doing surveillance on me, Max?"

I'd started to respond, and then thought better of it. Instead, I raised a finger indicating "wait a minute." Women like Sherry do not like fingers raised in their faces—hell, I don't like fingers raised in my face. But she waited.

The sergeant looked at Sherry, then at me, and flipped his notebook closed.

"You did say you'd be following up on this with the sheriff's office and Chief Hammonds, right, Detective?" he said. Sherry nodded.

"This may very well dovetail into an investigation under the chief's purview, Sergeant," she said. The sergeant tried unconvincingly not to roll his eyes.

"Very well, then. This is all most likely above my pay grade," he said, copying Sherry's official vernacular, a cant that is often used in law enforcement circles when someone is trying to cover his or her ass. "I'll be sure that a copy of my report is forwarded to the chief's attention. Good night, Detective."

The cops gathered their evidence and left us alone. It was time for me to atone for my raised finger. "I didn't mean to cut you off," I started.

"Yes you did."

"OK," I said. "I did."

I let that sit. Medicine, my mother used to say; take it.

"What I wanted to say, but only to you, was that we found a tracking device on my car, the Gran Fury, I mean. We think this guy has been tracking my movements, following wherever I went. A witness saw him at Billy's beach bungalow where we were keeping Luz Carmen."

"We think he planted a bomb under my car at the ranger station by the shack. And the gun they just took off of him was probably the gun that killed a pit bull at the firebombing of the trailer that killed Carmen's brother and girlfriend and her teenage son."

Only part of Sherry's face was illuminated in the light from the house. She was a tough woman, but not unforgiving.

"So you came racing down here to protect me." She didn't voice the *awww* that might come with such a statement—that particular expression was not in Sherry's vocabulary. But I knew what she meant.

"I tried to call," I said. "I left messages. I couldn't reach you."

"Did you call 911? Did you tell dispatch that a potential assassin might be at an officer's home?"

"No."

"Had to do it yourself, right, Max? Knight in shining armor stuff."

I looked straight out into the darkness. OK, the woman knew me— no wiggling out of it.

"But I did try to call . . ."

"I was out with Marty Booker," she said.

I turned to look at her face, the one that has never lied to me.

"He admitted the steroid drug use to me, Max. And he gave me the boxes that the stuff came in. I took the lot numbers to the guys who raided the warehouse and matched them up with the stuff they removed from the place. Booker and his friends were pipelined into the same operation. The Brown Man was supplying the drugs. When Booker got sick of it and told the rest of them he was getting out, that's when they turned the cold shoulder on him."

"And how long after that did he end up getting squashed in the accident on the I-595?" I said.

She was running the possible permutations in her head. I was doing them out loud.

"The Brown Man hired an assassin to clean up anyone who could lead back to him," I said. "He put the asshole onto everyone, including

Booker. The collision that crippled him was done by the same idiot they just hauled out of here."

Sherry was staring at me. Even in the dim light, I could see incredulity on her face, and Sherry does not do incredulity often. "Big supposition, Max."

I looked out on the pool water, the dark surface reflecting some of the ambient light, the small ripples from a breeze catching glints of it.

"He admitted it."

"The hit man?"

"Yeah. He named the Brown Man. He said Carlyle named the targets, and then paid him when it was done."

"Jesus, Max, how'd you get him to give that up?"

"Persuasion." I couldn't look up at her.

"The kind that causes unconsciousness and a knot on the back of the head?" she said.

"And probably a little chlorine in the lungs," I said, still looking away from Sherry's eyes.

Again, there was silence, but there wasn't a question in it, more a weighing of justice deserved or denied.

"They won't be able to use that in court," she finally said.

"They can flip him," I said. "A good prosecutor can use the attempted murder of a law enforcement officer to make that kid sing like an American Idol."

"That would be one legal way to do it," Sherry said, and the implication was clear.

"I'm not a cop; I'm a PI," I said, justifying.

She let that excuse sit for several beats, and then reached out and put her hand on top of mine.

"You're a good man, Max."

I waited as long as she had before answering.

"Sometimes," I said.

25

YOU SHOULD HAVE been smarter. But fuck it, man—this was the way it had been pointing all along, isn't it? You've been walking, ha, rolling, down this path, and now it comes to this.

"Marty, I don't know what to tell you," the blonde detective said after you spilled your guts.

Yeah, she did know what to tell you. She could have told you straight out that you'd broken the law. Cheated, did the steroids, bought illegal drugs, conspired with a known drug dealer, and broke your entire fucking covenant with the law enforcement community you'd always dreamed of being part of.

But it's always *what if*, isn't it?

Enough *what if*, Marty: You know what has to be done.

So when she left, you looked around the garage. You rolled down off the ramp and over to the counters, the ones you'd built with your own hands. You had measured the wood yourself, the thick oak, the kind that couldn't just be kicked in by some skinny dickweed breaking into your garage. You'd put on the heavy-duty hinges, double-drilled the stainless-steel hasps, and locked it down with a round cylinder stainless padlock. It was better than a safe 'cause no one would assume what it contained. Key it open, and there she is, the old Mossberg 500 your father gave to you before he died—and what better weapon to use, huh? Make your father proud, after all the fucking up you've done.

OK, you took her out of the cabinet and slipped the old carrying case off. She smelled like aged gun oil. It had been about two years since you last had her out and took her down to the range in Markham Park and did some skeet with a couple of the guys. You should have taken better care of her. Yeah, should've done a lot of the things.

It actually hurt your heart to take her and put her in the vise on the workbench, clamping her in hard right along the pump action. You could feel the nonslip pattern of the vise teeth sinking into the wood. When you took the hacksaw and started that cut on the barrel to bring it down to size, you could hear Daddy yelling, "Son, what the hell are you thinking?"

But this was the only way, wasn't it? Saw off the barrel and strip the shoulder stock to give her a kind of pistol grip. That's the way you'd be able to hide the shotgun along your leg in the wheelchair without drawing too much attention. The Brown Man might be a useless drug dealer, but he was also street smart. He'd probably seen a dozen competitors and pissed-off clients coming at him in the past, and knew what to look for. But a cripple cop loaded up with 00 buck? The man wouldn't know what hit him.

So you sanded off the rough metal at the working end of the barrel and loaded her with four shells, even though you knew you'd only need two. You wrapped her up in a black field jacket and then used the cell phone to call a cab. Hell, you had the number memorized by now. Even the daytime dispatcher knew your voice by now after all the times you'd called them. "Oh, yeah, the legless guy who has to have a ride to the beach for a workout at the gym, or down to Bootlegger's for a beer, or to Publix for a bag of microwave dinners."

Sure, the driver will just toss the chair in the trunk and then set it up by the back door. Then you can use your arms to wiggle your ass out and crawl into the seat.

"Yeah, thanks, pal, and here's a tip for helping out. I'd give you a twenty if you'd wipe my ass. Fuck it, I'm just kidding you, buddy, really, keep the change."

The driver had given you a strange look, like he wasn't sure if you were a smart ass or a whack job. And to tell the truth, you weren't sure yourself. When the cab finally dropped you off, there you were in front of the compound of Carlyle Carter, a.k.a. the Brown Man, in Northwest Fort Lauderdale, looking up at the white metallic gates and the surveillance cameras on the house.

You rolled your chair right up to the mounted intercom and punched the speaker button. Would the guy even answer? Hell, yes, you figured. This was someone who flaunted his shit. I mean, look at this place. Every cop in the county knew who lived here, and where the money came from to build it. The Brown Man couldn't help himself. He'd be too curious not to see you.

So when the melodious male voice came over the speaker—"Yes, may I help you?"—you flipped open your badge case with your sheriff's star and held it up for the camera.

"I need to speak to Carlyle Carter."

There was silence. But you stayed put, holding up the badge, the one you'd disgraced. The sawed-off shotgun was hard against your right hip. You were forty feet away from the man's front door. You kept your face as calm as possible, no hint of anger, no look of consternation, only what you thought of as a look that a determined businessman might wear.

Come on, fucker, you thought. Have some balls.

After five minutes of silence, you heard the front door of the house open and Carter stepped out, dressed in a bright white linen suit that you could never afford on your salary. Under his loose jacket, he wore a white shirt, buttoned tight at the collar, and white loafers that looked like golf shoes to you, but who the fuck knows? In the harsh sunlight, the getup seemed to glow, making the Brown Man's coffee-colored face appear to be floating as he moved carefully down the driveway. You were looking to see if he was armed, but the man's hands were deep into his loose trouser pockets and could have been concealing all but the largest of handguns. He stopped some thirty feet from the gate.

"It is unusual for police officers, especially simple foot patrolmen, to visit my private home, Mr. Booker," he said. If the use of the phrase *foot patrolmen* was a purposeful dig, his voice didn't show it. He looked back at his house, head tilted up toward the cameras.

"Most officers don't like the idea that they could be filmed here, and that such evidence could end up on a desk in your internal affairs division."

No shit, Sherlock, you thought. But you'd already practiced your response. The words felt dry and dirty in your mouth. Still, you got them out.

"I need your help, Mr. Carter," you said.

The Brown Man's eyebrows went up, a near imperceptible response. He took three casual steps closer.

"I would caution you, Mr. Booker," he said, cutting his eyes to the right where the intercom box was mounted. "There is a recording device that will also preserve everything you say."

But there wasn't anything you were going to say now that you hadn't already said to the blonde detective. It was already out there, man. Only one thing left to do: If this fuck wad would only come another twenty feet closer, it would be over. And that's when you saw the movement behind him, the Brown Man, someone else moving at the door to the house. Your hand moved down to your hip: You could blow this man away before some kind of bodyguard came out and capped you first.

The Brown Man turned at the look in your eye, turned to see what had pulled your attention. "Go back inside, Andrew!" Carter said. "This is nothing for you."

But the kid stepped out, the ten-year-old, the same one who'd made all those drug drops to you. He was dressed in the typical style of the day: long baggy shorts that came down to his calves, an oversize T-shirt, ball cap turned sideways on his head. His eyes were too calm and effortless for a kid that age, too "I don't give a shit" for a boy who would have a natural energy and inquisitiveness. The Mustang had brought that childlike joy in his eyes whenever the boy made a delivery.

Now it was more of a feral sizing up the situation. Hell, without your car, he might not recognize you at all, never mind without your legs.

"He's your son?" you said, not meaning to let the words slip out. The Brown Man turned back, and now his eyes were different, too.

"Not that's it's any of your business, Booker. But yes, he's my son. And the smartest employee I have. You have a problem with that?" Carter said, and you could tell you'd hit a live wire.

"You use your own son as a drug mule, a kid to make your deliveries?" you said without thinking, letting the emotion slip through. And instantly, you knew you'd lost the plan, lost the ruse to pull the man into a faux business deal that would ease his reluctance by appealing to his greed and bring him within range.

But he stepped forward anyway, this time with anger in his face.

"What, Mr. Dirty Cop? You're going to tell me how to raise my own son? You with the drug habit, you handing out the money that goes into my pockets, you with the tin shield—you think that makes you better than me?"

Hell, you couldn't have planned it this well: Carter getting pissed, coming closer, railing at you to make it that much easier to pull the trigger.

"Is that what your daddy taught you, Mr. Cripple? I teach my son how to survive, how to do business with the likes of you. His generation ain't so stupid if you show them the way of the world, Mr. Righteous Cop."

Our eyes met then, the Brown Man stepping close enough now that you could see the freckles on his dark face, the now damp stain on the collar of his white shirt, the anger pulsing in the vein at his neck.

Your hand was already on the makeshift grip of the shotgun. And when it came forward, barely three inches of the sawed-off barrel poked out of the jacket that hid it, and you shoved it forward between the rungs of the gate and fired nearly point-blank into the Brown Man's sternum. The blast echoed through the neighborhood, the 00 buckshot, nine large pellets, ripping through cloth and flesh and lung tissue and ruining the spotlessness of the man's suit with an instantaneous spread of red blood, like the snarling mouth of a rabid dog.

The man only took a short hop back, and then crumpled like a marionette suddenly cut loose of its strings. When the Brown Man fell onto the driveway pavement, you could see the son standing beyond him, his eyes wide and his mouth frozen.

You did not say a word—only pumped the shotgun once, heard the ejected shell hit the sidewalk, and then rotated the barrel so that the newly sanded aperture fit snug under your chin. Then you pulled the trigger once more.

26

WE GATHERED AT Billy's penthouse apartment overlooking the ocean in West Palm Beach. The moon was down, and there was a hint of a breeze coming in with the tide. Luz Carmen was out on the patio, looking out into the dark, listening to the hush of waves. We were not worried that she might throw herself over the railing.

Billy and his wife were on one of the leather loveseats in the sunken living room. They sat close, Billy sipping one of the martinis that he prided himself on making in the classic mode, dry, with the open bottle of vermouth only passed over the top of the vodka, allowing barely more than the aroma to insinuate the drink. Curiously, Diane was not imbibing as she usually would. Sherry and I were on the couch, sharing a bottle of Rolling Rock.

Billy's place has a museum quality about it: the African hand-carved ebony sculptures, a fascinating collection of Southwest paper clay art, and a stunning copy of *The Guardian of the Seraglio* by Eduard Charlemont dominating the southern wall. Billy once told me the sword-bearing chief depicted was said to guard the women in his Moorish palace.

When I looked from the painting to Billy, he showed no indication that he was reading my mind. But the allusion was not lost on me.

"Horace D. Wiggins is apparently s-singing an aria d-down at the Broward Sheriff's Office," Billy said, using the now known name of our "assassin."

"He's already admitted t-taking assignments from Carlyle Carter, the so-called Br-Brown Man, and seems quite enamored with himself as a real hit m-man. When he is charged with the m-murders of Andrés and his girlfriend, the attempted murders of Booker and of b-both of you, I suppose he will at some point realize that he can't just push the reset b-button on the game and start all over again."

"How old is he?" I said.

"Twenty."

The disappointment in Billy's voice was once again stronger than I was used to. "B-Barely more than a child himself. He'll see soon enough that the inside of a m-maximum-security prison is not nearly as intriguing as the television version."

"He admitted to setting the bomb under Max's car?" Sherry said.

"Apparently, the Medicare fraud people got nervous about one of their satellite operations. They shared their concern with Carter, and since it threatened his drug supply chain, Carter put word out on the street that he wanted the Carmen family scared into silence," I said.

"The shooters at the park and the gang who tried to hit Andrés from the car?" Diane asked.

"That's how you got involved," Sherry stated the obvious, a favorite dig of hers that referred to my recurring ability to get my ass in trouble.

"Wh-When that d-didn't work, our Mr. Carter w-went to his n-next line of defense. He p-put his young assassin on alert, and Mr. Wiggins began following his t-targets with GPS trackers that apparently were being pl-placed by Carter's own son at his father's instructions.

"They will m-match the fingerprint from the GPS found in the Gran Fury. Another child will go into the system."

I watched as Diane's free hand moved to cover Billy's. They had always been an affectionate couple since their marriage three years ago, but there was something else going on.

I turned to Sherry, passed the beer to her, and changed the subject.

"What about Booker?"

"His parents are coming down from New York to claim the body. His father is an ex-cop," Sherry said. "Not a good situation. He'll lose his pension. Probably be buried with no recognition from the office. I know some deputies who thought he did the world a favor by taking out Carter, but there are at least a few knuckleheads over at the Oceanside Gym who are sweating bullets right about now."

"You p-put in your report on what Booker told you?" Billy asked.

"Damn straight," she said. "Hammonds will roll some heads."

"And all without so much as lifting a finger," I said.

Sherry took a sip of the bottle and laughed.

"That's what he has you for, Max."

"He played me," I admitted.

"That's what a good manager does when his manpower is down in a bad economy. He uses good freelancers—doesn't have to pay benefits."

"Law enforcement follows a b-business model," Billy said, tipping his martini glass.

"Damn straight," I said, mocking Sherry.

"You're both full of shit," Diane said, but she was smiling.

"That may be true," I said. "But since we're on the subject, what happens to the other criminals in this entire cluster that started the whole thing—the guys running the Medicare scam? The guys making the big bucks behind their computers and paperwork and licensing and stolen social security numbers . . ."

We all looked at one another, trading eye contact, avoiding the fact that we had no ready answers.

"The wheels of justice grind slowly, M-Max," Billy finally said.

"Hah!" I sputtered. "Some things never change, eh?"

But Billy's eyes went over to his wife, the judge.

A hush fell over the room as I got up to fetch another beer. When I asked Sherry if she'd share it, she declined. So I opened a bottle from Billy's big stainless fridge and eased outside onto the patio.

"Can I get you anything, Ms. Carmen?"

Luz Carmen was quiet. I wasn't sure she'd heard me. I thought she might have fallen asleep. But then she said, "The ocean tides, they change every day, but then, they never really change year after year, do they, Mr. Freeman?

I stepped forward and put a hand on the railing. It was dark to the east, but if you listened carefully, you could hear the soft surf below.

The feds never did show up at the ranger station to put Luz in protective custody. Billy had instead taken her to his place. When I called him after the arrest of our "assassin" at Sherry's, the threat was deemed to have been minimized. After we found out about the murder of the Brown Man and suicide of Deputy Booker, we had to reluctantly agree.

Two days later, Luz arranged a cremation of her brother's remains, held a simple service, and prayed, I supposed, to her own private god. Afterward, she told Billy that she would be returning to Bolivia.

I didn't know how to respond to her rumination on the human lack of change.

She was emotionally wounded, unsure what direction to take, beaten down by the turns her life had taken. It was familiar territory for me. I'd been there a few years ago when I chose to pick up and leave Philadelphia for South Florida.

"But you know, the tides also go in and out, Ms. Carmen. They rise and fall, just like life."

"Ah, the philosopher Mr. Freeman," she said, a hint of amusement in her voice for the first time since I'd met her.

"No," I said. "The realist."

She let that sit for a moment. "Fair enough," she finally said. "I will be returning to my true home."

"Bolivia?"

"Yes, to Rurrenabaque," she said. "The short time out in your Everglades has convinced me that I might find peace there. I may have relatives who will help. I may be able to teach there—maybe English to the children."

Only one side of her face was illuminated in the darkness. She was again looking out at something I could not see.

"The place of the pink dolphins?" I said, and this time she actually smiled.

"Yes. It is the one place where I remember my brother being a true child, an innocent."

If all she had left were memories, I wasn't going to deny her that respite. I did not respond and drifted quietly back into the apartment. Two steps in, I looked up and was instantly aware of a thickness of anticipation.

Sherry turned to me, smiling as if she'd been missing me for days. Billy was looking askance, as if some joke had gone awry. But his wife was glowing, her eyes bright, and her complexion somewhere between an embarrassed flush and deep pride. They had all frozen with my entrance, as if they'd popped a bottle of champagne, and were waiting for the cork to hit something.

"Diane and Billy are having a baby!" Sherry said.

I suffered the instant of silence such a statement deserves, and blurted out something like, "What? How?"

Sherry waved her fingers at me the way she does when I make a bad joke, and then performed an impressive, one-legged stand-up to meet Diane in a hug.

I strode across to Billy and took his extended hand. "Congratulations, Counselor," I said, hoping the tone in my voice did not reveal the question that next rang in my head: Is this something you really want?

The ensuing gush of conversation was of due dates and maternity time and the clearing out of an extra bedroom, and then a belated, in my opinion, call for real champagne. Crystal flutes appeared and a chilled bottle, and whether in deference to Luz Carmen, or simply because Billy's particular taste doesn't not call for exploding corks, the wine was carefully opened and poured.

Diane accepted half a glass. "For celebration only," she said. "I'll have to get used to giving this up."

After the toast, the ritualistic separation of the genders occurred. The women huddled together in their particular sharing of stories and questions, and the men drifted off under the confident gaze of the Moorish guard mounted on the wall.

"This is what's been bugging you lately?" I said, not bothering to list the times Billy had shown uncharacteristic anger during the last few days, and the profound disappointment on his face when the circumstances of young people, children, had been revealed.

"It is a difficult w-world today, Max," Billy said. "I would not tr-try to deceive you b-by pretending that I haven't given thought to bringing a child into it. Children who grow up without direction, children who grow up without any worthy role models; worse, children who are actually taught the kind of selfishness and manipulation, and outright lawlessness by the ones they depend on most."

I could not argue with him. Billy had grown up without a father. I had grown up in the shadow of domestic violence. But somehow we made it out, hadn't we? Still, it was a different time.

"I have heard the argument, my friend, that if people like you and Diane, smart and carrying people of high morals and strong ethics don't bring children into this world, then we are all lost," I said.

I raised the edge of my glass to his and lightly touched them together. "At this moment in time, Billy, I think we need you."

27

THE RIDE HOME was quiet, as you might expect after the resolution of a case, the Manchesters' announcement of a child on the way, and the simmering non-resolution of something that still stood in the way of my relationship with Sherry.

"Isn't that great about Billy and Diane?"

"Yeah, great."

"What? You're not happy for them?"

"Sure, I'm happy. If that's what they want—and they know what they're getting into with all the time and attention and dedication involved in raising a kid—which I'm sure they do. Then it's great."

Quiet. The spaced lights along I-95 set up an almost metronome quality as they strobed through the truck at sixty-five m.p.h., whisking over the hood, onto the dashboard, the quick glow on both our faces, and then gone until the next one.

"It's not always just about the commitment and the dedication and the responsibility, Max," Sherry said.

I nodded.

"It's also about the love."

Sherry unbuckled her seat belt, rolled on one hip, and rested her head on my shoulder.

"You know that's illegal, Detective?" I said, moving the back of my fingers to her cheek.

"So arrest me."

When we got to her house, the street was once again staid, neat, dark, and quiet. Wind ruffled the trees. The scent of night-blooming jasmine tickled the air. Sherry didn't wait for me to unload the wheelchair. On occasion, she acquiesced to using her aluminum forearm crutches for short distances.

"Meet me out back," she said over her shoulder, and went inside.

I took out the wheelchair and went through the side gate and pulled the contraption backward up onto the deck. The pool lights were on. We'd had an electrician come to repair and recheck all the lines. There was something about that blue-green glow that I'd missed when it wasn't there, and I'd actually wondered why complete darkness never bothered me out at the shack, but I avoided it here.

I went inside to the kitchen and took a couple of beers out of the fridge. Sherry was still in the back somewhere, so I opened the Rolling Rocks and returned to the deck. Sitting at the patio table, I watched the lights dance off the oak leaves and the tile around the pool, and then— almost unconsciously—off the chrome of the wheelchair.

Without examining my thought process, I got up and moved the chair, rolling it back behind Sherry's hammock in the corner, where it was out of sight. I had just settled back into my chair when the pool lights went out.

"It's OK, Max," Sherry said from the French doors of her bedroom, before I had a chance to jump. The still, burning light behind her showed her in silhouette. She was moving across the patio with the forearm crutches, and when she passed me, I felt the bare skin of her hip touch my shoulder. The scent of jasmine was replaced by a perfume I had not smelled for more than a year.

I heard the ruffle of water as Sherry lowered herself into the pool, and I hesitated for only a second. My heart was thumping when I stepped naked into the water and found her in the dark.

There is something about water, its movement, its cocoon of film over skin, its ability to mimic weightlessness: Some call it limbic; some call it internal; some call it healing. We used no words at all.

Later, when I carried Sherry to her bedroom and lay her down on the bed, I noticed that the mirror she had depended on for so long was gone. She had moved it from its regular space, stored it away perhaps for good.

We lay in each other's arms for hours that night, neither sleeping, nor dreaming.

"Thank you, Max," Sherry finally said.

"For?" I whispered.

"For saving me."

I used my fingertips to move a strand of her hair behind her ear and watched her profile against the glow from the pool.

"Then I thank you, for the same reason, babe," I said.

She turned to meet my eyes and whispered a phrase for the ages before meeting my lips with hers:

"Saving each other, Max—isn't that what people are supposed to do?"

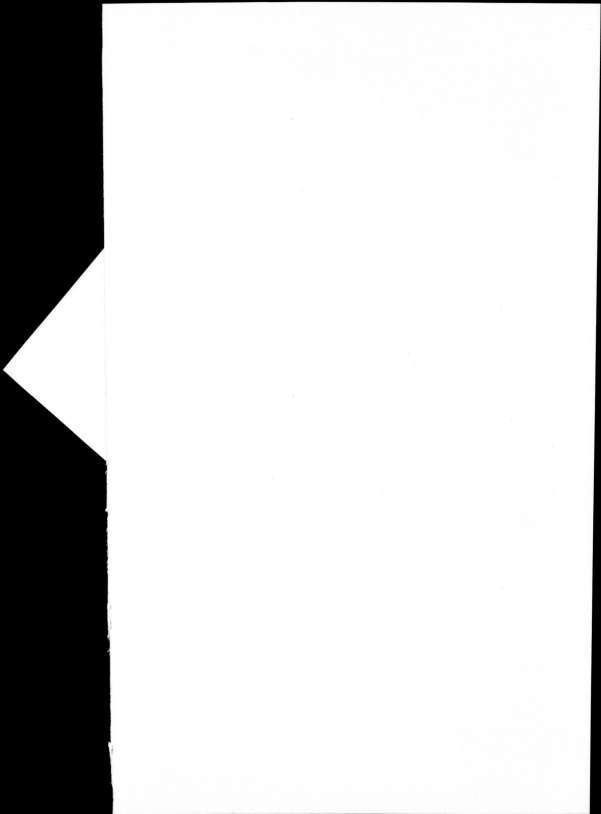

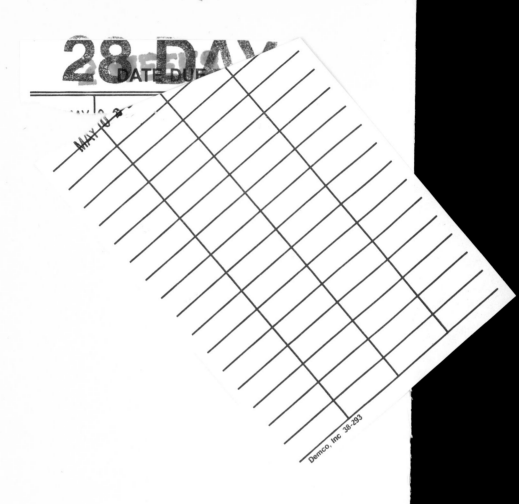

King, Jonathon.

Midnight guardians